Ebony and Ivory

Ebony and Ivory

David Morgan Williams

THE SPIRIT OF THE DRAGON

– A Celtic Odyssey

Book 1 – Dragonrise

Book 2 – Ebony and Ivory

First impression: 2007
© David Morgan Williams and Y Lolfa Cyf., 2007

*This book is subject to copyright
and may not be reproduced by any means
except for review purposes
without the prior written consent of the publishers*

Cover design: Y Lolfa

ISBN: 0 86243 972 8
ISBN-13: 978 0 86243 972 9

Printed on acid-free and partly recycled paper
and published and bound in Wales by
Y Lolfa Cyf., Talybont, Ceredigion SY24 5AP
e-mail ylolfa@ylolfa.com
website www.ylolfa.com
tel 01970 832 304
fax 832 782

Dedication

To my very special grandchildren, who seem to be growing up so quickly: Josh, Joe, Sam, Jake, Matt, Molly and Tim.

And to children throughout this troubled world whose lives are being blighted, and in some cases devastated, by the evil forces of terrorism.

May God bless them, for they are all our futures!

Acknowledgements

To my loving wife Jan for putting up with my endless chatter about plots and sub-plots, for sparking off a new idea, and for just being there!

My loving appreciation to my daughter Ceri for typing a large part of the typescript, and for motivating me to complete the unfinished work on this story.

My sincere thanks to my son-in-law Keith who has patiently guided me through the swamp of 'computer-speak', and the Aladdin's cave of computer gizmos.

My gratitude to my son Chris and his wife Kath for introducing me to 'Dragon Naturally Speaking' voice technology, and other technical help whenever needed.

Many thanks to my eldest grandson Josh for designing and drawing the 'Dragon with Open Book' logo for the 'Spirit of the Dragon' series. May this be the first of many successes for him in the years to come!

To my daughter Megs for her invaluable help with the graphics.

I acknowledge the magical quotes from C. S. Lewis to Shakespeare which appear at the beginning of my story, all of which have inspired me during my writing.

Finally, my sincere thanks once again to my editor Lefi Gruffudd and his staff at Y Lolfa for their continuing support and skill in the publishing of this book. Pob Hwyl!

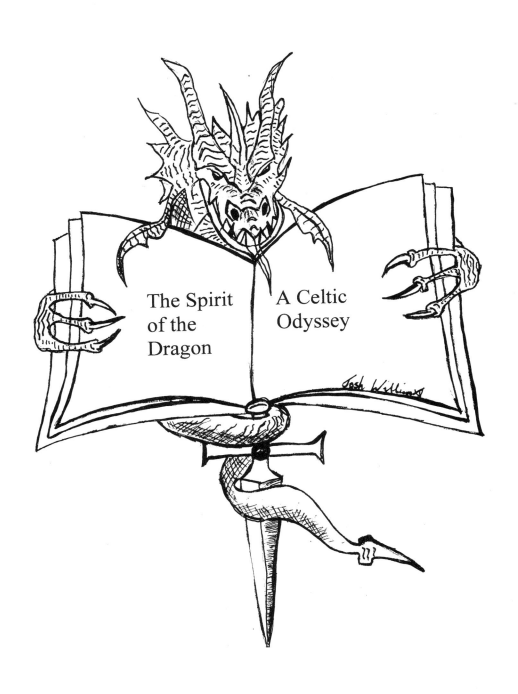

So Pwyll went to sit on top of a hill called the throne of Aberth, and a woman came riding by on a grey-white horse and wearing silk the colour of bright gold. Pwyll mounted his fastest horse and forced it to go as fast as it could, but the greater the haste the further she was from him ... then he called out, "Lady, for the sake of the one you love most, wait for me."

"I'll wait gladly," she replied.

> *Pwyll – Prince of Dyfed, Tales from The Mabinogion*, translated by Gwyn Thomas and Kevin Crossley-Holland, and illustrated by Margaret Jones, 1992

When he felt the Ebony Horse move under him, and then rise in the air, the Prince was filled with great joy. Never in all his years of hunting had he travelled so fast or seen as far as now. Thus he passed over mountains and deserts, oceans and forests, even to the boundaries of China.

> *The Tale of the Ebony Horse*, from *The Arabian Nights*, translated by Brian Alderson, and illustrated by Michael Foreman, 1992

The horse was revered in the Celtic World for its beauty, speed, and sexual vigour, and this animal became a symbol of the aristocratic warrior-elite of Celtic society ... the Knights.

> *Epona and Horses*, from *Celtic Myths* by Miranda Jane Green 1993

The Horse, the horse! The symbol of surging potency and power of movement, and of action, in man.

> D H Lawrence

"A horse, a horse! My Kingdom for a horse!"

Richard 1II, *Act 2, Scene 2, L.156,*
William Shakespeare, 1591

The best horses become like your best friends; you can rely on them when you need them most.

On the retirement of Shamardal,
Frankie Dettori, *The Times*, 2.7.05

Perhaps it has happened to you in a dream, that someone says something which you don't understand, but in the dream it feels as if it has enormous meaning – either a terrifying one which turns the whole dream into a nightmare or else a lovely meaning too lovely to put into words, which makes the dream so beautiful that you remember it all your life and are always wishing you could get into that dream again. It was like that now.

The Lion, the Witch and the Wardrobe,
C.S.Lewis, 1950

And in this life, nothing GOOD is truly lost. It stays part of a person, and becomes part of their character.

The Shell Seekers.
Rosamunde Pilcher, 2000

The Story so far…

In *Dragonrise* (Book 1), Huw Pendry, a 12-year-old schoolboy, lives in the Welsh Borderland (the Marches). As the story unfolds it soon becomes evident that Huw is in a state of inner turmoil. His mother, Beth, a policewoman, has recently been killed, while attempting to arrest a group of men who had broken into a local armaments factory. He is highly vulnerable and sensitive to what is happening around him, and especially the disturbances taking place at the ancient burial mound, TWMP TRELECH, (the Mound with 3 Standing Stones), which is situated close to Pendry Farm that belongs to his Uncle Mog.

He sets off, one stormy night, to meet his cousin Arthur, who lives at the farm, but the weather conditions are so bad that he falls from his mountain bike and bangs his head on a rock. When he regains consciousness, a strange force draws him towards the mound, and he soon finds himself face to face with the Guardian Spirit of the mound, a Dragon with a monstrously big yellow eye. He is mesmerized by the eye, and afterwards is able to recount his experience only in brief flashes, which are largely disbelieved by those he tells his story to, including his cousin Arthur and his friend Samantha.

However, as the story unfolds, he discovers that the men who killed his mother are using the burial mound as a hideout, and a place to hide the stolen weapons and explosives. Their Leader, Kervlan, is a ruthless terrorist, who will stop at nothing to achieve his evil ends, and those of a Global Terrorist Group of which he is a part.

Huw, Arthur, and Sam, with a lot of help from the Dragon Spirit, eventually overcome enormous odds to defeat this cell of terrorists, but they had no way of knowing that the real conflict was only just beginning.

Now read on ...

Chapter 1

Sandstorm

"Where am I?" groaned Huw.

As he slowly regained consciousness, he felt a massive jolt shudder through his body.

"Arghh!" he cried out, as a searing pain shot from the top of his head, down his neck and into his trembling limbs. His wrists and ankles were bound, and the ropes cut deeply into his flesh.

"Stop, stop!" he pleaded as the open-backed vehicle in which he was travelling bounced and jolted along the dirt track road. His body rolled wildly from side to side, but as he slowly opened his eyes he could see that he was securely tethered to a steel ring in the floor of the truck. His cries of pain were stifled by the rising wind and the sand and stones that rattled like machine gun bullets against the underbelly of the truck. Clouds of choking dust swirled around him and he strained on his ropes in an effort to seek more shelter. A heavy tarpaulin hung from the back of the cab, Huw struggled and squirmed until he managed to force his head beneath it. He began to breathe more easily, but the struggle had sapped his strength and he suddenly felt faint and nauseous, and once again, he sank into oblivion.

* * *

As the truck hurtled onwards at breakneck speed, Huw's head throbbed in time with the truck's heavy-throated engine. He began to see brief flashbacks of what had happened just an hour earlier, as he was abruptly woken from a deep sleep by the shrill cry of a horse in distress. He saw himself scrambling out of bed and pulling on his tracksuit and trainers. Still half asleep, he opened his bedroom door and scuttled down the long corridor leading to the great sweeping staircase. He clung on to the marble balustrade to steady himself. Then, when he reached the bottom, he dashed across the hallway. He tripped on one of his flying laces and fell flat on his face. He cursed beneath his breath as he pulled himself up into a sitting position and tied his laces. He took a few seconds to rub his bruised knees and elbows, and then moved quickly towards the heavy main door. He heaved against the door and managed to open it just enough for him to squeeze through, almost falling over the body of the unconscious Captain of the Guard. Now, he knew that something was seriously wrong, and he ran across the Palace courtyard towards the stables.

The wind was rising, and small sand grains began to sting his face. The courtyard was deserted, and there were no guards to be seen. As he hurried on he heard the sounds of restless horses coming from the stable block. He stopped suddenly, and felt very afraid. He was tempted to go back to the palace for help, but the sounds of distress drove him on.

He was breathing hard now, and he had a pain in his side. As he drew near to the stables the whole area was plunged into darkness. Someone has cut off the power supply, Huw thought to himself, as he lifted his left arm to shield his face from the stinging sand. He saw faint pin-points of light flickering on and off in the stables. He heard the sound of cascading water to his left, and realized he was passing the courtyard fountains. He paused for a moment, to splash the cooling water over his face, and clear the sand from his eyes. He stumbled on towards the faint lights, and gradually he could see that the main gate to the stables was open. His heart was pounding as he crept slowly towards the open gate. He heard something move behind him, but as he turned he felt a sharp blow to the head. The pain was intense. He slumped to the floor, and darkness enveloped him.

* * *

A sudden jolt brought Huw back to the present, and his body ached with pain. The truck was still being driven recklessly. As he came to, he could make out a large, dark shape swinging back and fore behind him. The truck was pulling a horse-box. The horses were whimpering as they were thrown around in the box. Huw felt a surge of anger rising within him. How could anyone be so cruel, and treat animals in this way? Who were these evil people, and why were they doing this? A stabbing pain shot through his head, and in the semi-darkness beneath the tarpaulin, he saw blood dripping onto the floor of the truck. He knew he was badly hurt, but there was nothing he could do except hang on until the nightmare was over. If it ever would be. What he didn't know then was that the nightmare was just beginning.

Chapter 2

Smokescreen

Five minutes after Huw had been awoken, Arthur was disturbed by the distant growl of a diesel engine starting up. He crossed over to his bedroom window and saw a dust cloud rising from a truck as it swept through the open gates of the stables, a horse box swaying alarmingly behind it. It sped off into the desert as Arthur grabbed his clothes and ran out into the corridor. Huw's bedroom door was open but there was no sign of him. Arthur ran to Sam's bedroom, threw open the door and yelled to her that something was badly wrong over at the stables, and he was going to investigate. By the time he reached the top of the stairs, Sam was behind him, struggling into her tracksuit.

"Look," shouted Arthur, "the door leading into the courtyard is open, and there's someone lying on the floor outside."

"Is it Huw?" cried Sam.

"Can't see from here. Come on, quick!"

They leapt down the stairs and scurried across the hallway to the main doors.

"It's not Huw," said Arthur.

"Then, who is it?"

"It's Captain Maktar of the Palace guard," said Arthur.

"He's hurt," said Sam, as she heard the Captain groan. She bent over him and gasped, there was blood all over his face.

"Go quickly," said the captain, pointing towards the stables, "or it will be too late to save the horses."

"But you are wounded," said Sam, in alarm.

"I will live," said the Captain. "Please go quickly."

The Captain gave them no choice, so Arthur and Sam ran across the courtyard, which by now was filled with swirling dust and something else too. An acrid smell filled their nostrils.

"It's smoke," cried Arthur, "and, look, there's a fire in the stables!"

As they got nearer, they began to realize the full horror of what was happening. The main stable doors were open and swinging wildly in the gusting wind. Smoke was billowing from the rear end of the stables, and the horses were shifting restlessly. Their hooves clattered against the stable doors as they tried to escape the fire. The stable guards were lying helpless on the floor.

"Try to open as many doors as you can," shouted Arthur, "but stand clear as the horses come out. They're very scared and will bolt as soon as they can see a way out."

Arthur was dead right; the horses bolted through the open gates and into the desert beyond. Sam could see the fear in their eyes, as they swept past them across the courtyard. There were dozens of thoroughbred horses in the Palace stables, all belonging to the Sheikh. That is, all except one – Mary Grant's horse.

"Arthur," shouted Sam, "I can't see any sign of Mum's horse."

"She must be here somewhere! Where was she stabled?" Arthur yelled against the rising wind and the swirling smoke.

"At the far end," said Sam, feeling a sense of panic rising up inside her, "but that's where the worst of the fire is. We can't go in there."

"Wait here," shouted Arthur, as he ran back towards the fountains in the Palace courtyard. He soaked his track suit top in the water and ran back to the stables. He wrapped the wet garment around his head and staggered towards the rear stable door. The heat was fierce, and he could feel the hot blast even through the wet cloth. He burned his hands as he threw open the bolts on the stable door. As he pulled them open, a great cloud of smoke billowed through the opening and was sucked out of the building into the night air. Arthur gasped.

"What is it?" cried Sam.

"There's nothing in there," said Arthur. "Your Mum's horse is gone."

"Oh, no!" cried Sam, "not Ivory!"

"Yes, and that's not all," groaned Arthur, "the fire's getting out of control."

Chapter 3

The Bedouin Boy

"What is it, Abu?" grumbled Ahmed, as he sat propped up against a date palm. "Can't you let me close my eyes for a few seconds without barking at me? What is it now?"

Ahmed stirred as his dog nudged him with his nose and then began gnawing at his sandals. The sheep and goats, too, were becoming restless. It was his turn on night watch, but he felt so tired after the day's exertions. Abu continued to worry him, and refused to stop barking.

"Oh, all right, I suppose I'd better see what's wrong," said Ahmed. He got to his feet and pulled his *farwa* (a sheepskin coat) tightly around him. Little goose bumps stood up on his skin as the cold night air caused him to shiver. He tugged his *abaya* (a black cloak) over his head for more protection.

"It's not just the cold, is it, Abu? There's something else wrong, isn't there? But what is it?"

Abu continued to bark and run round in circles, before dashing off down the hillside. From his vantage point on the hillside, Ahmed could see the Hajar Mountains rising thousands of feet behind him to the north and east. Away to the west and south lay the great desert plain, stretching far into the distance. Abu was still running down towards the plain, trying hard to draw Ahmed's attention.

Then, Ahmed saw what all the fuss was about. Far away on the horizon, a large dust cloud was forming and moving slowly towards him. He shouted to Abu that he had seen it. Why hadn't he noticed it before? He began to round up the sheep and goats, and move them back towards their compound on the edge of the Bedouin encampment. With Abu's help, he moved the animals quickly, until he could see the tents in the distance.

"Sheba, Sheba!" he called out, "there's a dust storm coming in this direction. Run as fast as you can and warn the others, quickly!"

Ahmed's younger sister heard the call, and ran swiftly towards the Bedouin tents. They must house the animals in the compound, and secure everything, before the sandstorm struck. She called out as she ran, and soon dozens of nomads emerged from their tents.

"Sandstorm! Sandstorm!" shouted Sheba. "Ahmed needs help with the animals! Secure your tents! The dust cloud is moving fast."

As soon as the animals were safe in the compound near the oasis, Ahmed and Abu returned to the hillside. He climbed higher, so that he had a better view of the approaching storm. The once clear night sky was now filling with a dark, boiling cloud, which completely filled the horizon. From where he stood, it looked to Ahmed like an enormous tidal wave. But this was dust not water.

Then, he noticed a pair of lights twinkling in the far distance, just on the edge of the rolling cloud. As the lights came closer, he began to realize that they were the powerful headlights of a large (4x4) desert truck. These trucks were specially built to drive in desert conditions, and had powerful diesel engines and large wheels with massive tyres. Behind the truck, he could see a horsebox, swaying alarmingly from side to side.

"You can see it too Abu, can't you?" said Ahmed, as his dog began barking once more. "The truck must be travelling very fast if it's going to out-run the storm. But why is it towing a horse-box at this time of night? Doesn't make sense; there's something strange going on out there."

Ahmed crouched low as the wind began to rise. The storm was drawing nearer at incredible speed. It seemed as if the whole desert floor was being sucked up into the sky. Millions of grains of sand were on the move, like liquid mountains.

"They're heading for the mountain road Abu," Ahmed shouted, as the wind began to howl and whine through the scrub and rock crevices of the foothills. He tried to keep his eyes focused on the truck as it lurched dangerously up the winding road, the driver struggling to keep just ahead of the smothering dust cloud. Ahmed looked up at the jagged mountain peaks above him, and right near the summit stood the ruins of the old stone fortress.

"Looks like that's where they're heading, Abu ... the old, forbidden fortress of Fujairah. Come on. Let's get back to camp, while we can still see where we're going."

Ahmed gasped as the choking dust began to engulf him. He crouched low and scrambled forward on all fours, as he copied Abu and kept just below the underbelly of the swirling cloud. At times like this, he was so glad to have his faithful dog with him. He knew that Abu would never leave his side, no matter what happened, and he also seemed to possess extra senses, which humans did not have. Ahmed had to make it back to camp, to tell what he had seen, but would he survive the suffocating sandstorm?

Chapter 4

The Prison

"Dad?" Nothing. "Arthur?" Nothing.

He called these names automatically, without thinking, because he could remember nothing else. Huw's weak calls echoed back from bare stone walls. He blinked hard and tried to focus on his surroundings. The blow to his head had given him blurred vision, but there was very little light anyway. What light there was came from a tiny open window high up in one corner of the small room in which he found himself. It was well out of reach, and in any case he was too weak to lift himself up off the floor, where he was lying on a thin straw mattress. He shivered, partly from the cold night air, and partly from the fever brought on by his injuries and the terrible journey which he had endured.

"Where am I?" he moaned. "What is this place? Why am I here?"

It must be early morning, he thought, as a thin shaft of light came through the tiny window. There was just enough light for him to see the bare stone walls of his cell. He threw off the coarse blanket which covered him, and struggled to his feet. As he drew himself up his head throbbed and he felt dizzy and nauseous. The room began to spin around and he reached out to the nearest wall, to steady himself. He ran his fingers over the surface of the stone until he felt small spaces where he could get a grip and cling to something solid. He clung then for what seemed like hours, until the dizziness passed and his vision cleared.

"Somebody, please help," he cried. "There must be some mistake! I'm not supposed to be here! I should be in …?"

Where was he supposed to be? He had no idea. His mind was blank. He had a terrifying feeling that he was all alone and that no-one could hear him.

Then, the sound of a horse neighing, far away, brought something back to his memory. He had sudden glimpses of the back of a truck as it lurched along the roughly surfaced road. He saw the horse box swinging wildly behind.

"Horses, horses, why am I hearing horses?"

Tears welled up in his eyes as he fought to remember what had happened in the night, and in the days before, but his mind was blank.

He groped his way around the rough stone walls and came to a large, iron door. He felt all around it, but there was no handle. It was locked from the other side. He banged on the door with his fists, but the metallic sounds reverberated around his small cell, and must have fallen on deaf ears on the outside because there was no response.

"Is there anybody there?" he cried. "Please let me out. I'm not supposed to be here!"

But where am I supposed to be? he thought. He couldn't

remember who he was, or where he was, only that there was some connection with horses. Once more, he heard the cry of the horse in the distance. The sound came through the small, open window above him, but he could not reach it, only look up and see the light.

"The light, yes, I remember the light, it was a bright, blazing light, a powerful light that drew me to it. It was a fire, that's right, a fire. But where was that? It must have been a dream."

Huw was rambling now, and hallucinating. He thought someone was in the cell with him, but he was only talking to himself. He was delirious. I wish the light was brighter in here, he thought. At least I would be able to see the details of this room more clearly.

"No, what am I saying? It's not a room at all; it's a cell, a dungeon. That's it, a dungeon. Then, I must be in prison! Help, somebody, help me. I'm not supposed to be here, I should be staying as a guest at the ...?"

Why did he say that? Was he a guest somewhere, but he couldn't remember? But why was he now a prisoner in this horrible place? He sank down onto the cold stone floor, his body shuddering with pain and his heart filled with anguish and fear. A stabbing pain shot down his neck from his head. He lifted his right hand and gingerly touched the wound on his head. It was matted with blood. He half remembered someone hitting him from behind, but then everything went black. Where had he been when this happened? He struggled to think, but it was to no avail. He was so weak, and he fell to the floor unconscious.

Chapter 5

Raising the alarm

"Run back to the Palace, Sam, raise the alarm, and tell Mike we can't find Huw," shouted Arthur, above the roaring flames, as the fire began to spread.

"Two of us will never bring this lot under control. I'll try and find a fire extinguisher; there must be one here somewhere."

Arthur was now breathing heavily and coughing, and his eyes were streaming and stinging from the smoke. Sam was already running. "I'll be back as soon as I can find help," she shouted.

The light from the fire illuminated the Palace courtyard, causing weird shapes to dance before her. Plumes of smoke snaked around the fountains and palm trees, like dark fingers, clawing at her legs as if they had some sinister motive to prevent her reaching the Palace.

"Captain Maktar!" she shouted as she reached the Palace doors, "are you all right?"

He had regained consciousness and was now in a sitting position, holding his head in his hands.

"I'll be all right in a short while," he said weakly.

"I will bring help right away," said Sam.

"Thank you," replied the Captain, "but, first, you must set the fire alarms ringing in the Palace. You will find them in the hallway and the main corridors. Break the glass and set off as many as you can. They will still function, despite the power cut."

Sam ran quickly into the hallway and saw the first alarm near the bottom of the staircase. She smashed the glass, and then covered her ears with her hands as the sound was deafening. Then, she followed the main marble corridor, with its high arched windows, through which she could see the flames getting higher above the stable block.

"Oh, Arthur," she cried, "hang on. Help is coming." Tears welled up in her eyes as she thought of Arthur battling alone against the fierce flames. And where was Huw? What had happened to him? How was she going to tell his Dad? As she set off another fire alarm, Amahl appeared from nowhere. He was the Sheikh's personal bodyguard, a large, burly figure of a man, with dark, fiery eyes and a large, black moustache.

"Is the fire in the stables?" asked Amahl, staring through the windows.

"Yes, and Arthur's there alone, trying to fight it. He needs help urgently. The night guards have been attacked and are either dead or injured, and Captain Maktar is recovering from the attack, outside the main entrance."

He hammered on a large door near the bottom of the stairs, and two men appeared, sleepy-eyed and in their nightshirts. Sam recognized them as the Sheikh's chauffeurs, Shakra and Nasra.

"There's a fire in the stables," shouted Amahl. "I am going to phone the emergency services and warn Sheikh Rashid. Can you rouse the rest of the Palace staff right away, and send every able-bodied man to the stable block."

As Amahl began dialling on his mobile phone, Sam turned and saw her mother Mary, and her new stepfather Henry Grant, at the foot of the stairs. She ran towards them with open arms.

"Oh, Mum," she cried, "there's a terrible fire at the stables. Arthur's there on his own, trying to stop it spreading."

"Where's Huw?" Mary asked, looking alarmed.

"I don't know. He's disappeared. He wasn't in his bedroom and we couldn't find him. Something dreadful's happened; I know it has!"

"I'll go to Arthur," said Henry. "Try to find Huw's Dad, and see if he knows where Huw is. Will you come with me, Amahl?"

"Of course; let's go."

Mary put her arm around Sam's shoulders, to comfort her. She could feel her body trembling with shock and fear.

"Come on back upstairs. You need a drink and some dry clothes."

"There's something else, Mum. It's not only Huw who's missing, Ivory's gone, too!"

"Ivory! Oh no, that can't possibly be … not Ivory … but why? All the horses were well guarded at night; how could anyone have got into the stables, or the Palace grounds, for that matter?"

"All the guards were lying on the ground, Mum, and Arthur thought they might have been gassed."

"Come on, Sam, I'll call the maidservants straight away. They'll take good care of you, while I go and find Huw's Dad."

As they climbed the long, winding staircase, Mary called out the servants names. "Lily, Rose, Daisy, please come quickly, we need your help."

The three Filipino maidservants appeared in an instant and took hold of Sam, who was now very weak and sinking at the knees.

"Please, take her to her room and look after her," said Mary, "and call a doctor if necessary. I must go and find Huw's father right away. Something awful may have happened to him. Would you come with me Rose, to help me find him? Do you know which room Mr Pendry is staying in?'

"Yes, Ma'am, I know where his room is. Come quickly!"

Rose scurried along the first floor corridor, with Mary following close on her heels. "The room is right down the end of the corridor, Ma'am, through many fire-doors, but we will get there soon."

When they arrived at Mike's door, Rose knocked loudly several times, but there was no reply.

"Try the master-key, Rose," said Mary. "I don't think Mr Pendry will mind, under the circumstances."

Rose unlocked the door and they both went inside. There was no sign of Mike, and the bed looked as if it hadn't been slept in. Mary walked across to the bedside and picked up a note in Mike's handwriting. It said that he had gone to visit Mr Saaed Ali, the Sheikh's chief Horse Trainer, at the Nadd Al Shiba racecourse, and he would be staying overnight with him. There was also a telephone number, where he could be reached in an emergency.

"Now, I remember," said Mary. "He mentioned yesterday that he might be staying overnight with Mr Ali. With all this turmoil going on, I had totally forgotten. I'll phone this number right away,

Rose. Let's pray we can get through."

As she dialled the number, Mary began to have the most terrible thoughts flashing through her mind. What if Huw was lying injured in the desert somewhere? A look of horror appeared in her eyes. Mike had already lost his wife Beth, in a shooting incident a year ago; what if he now lost his son too? The thought was unbearable and tears began to stream down her cheeks. Rose put her arms around her shoulders to comfort her.

"Don't cry, please, Ma'am … everything might be alright … we must pray that it will be."

The telephone crackled in Mary's hand, and she heard a man's voice at the other end of the line.

"Is that you, Mike? Oh, Mike, something dreadful has happened here during the night." Mary sobbed bitterly.

The man spoke again, but he had a strong Arabian accent.

"Hello, is that Mrs Grant? This is Mr Saeed Ali speaking. What has happened, please?"

"I'm so sorry, Mr Ali, but I need desperately to speak with Mr Pendry. I believe his son is in grave danger. May I speak with him urgently, please?"

"But, Mr Pendry is not here. He did not arrive for our appointment last night, and I was unable to reach him on the phone. I assumed he had a more urgent appointment. Please tell me what has happened at the Palace."

Mary tried to pull herself together, and in between sobs, told Mr Ali what had happened … the fire in the stables … Huw was missing … the horses were scattered in the desert.

"I am so sorry to hear this, Mrs. Grant, and I will alert all the staff at the racecourse immediately. If there is anything we can do, rest assured it will be done."

"Thank you so much, Mr Ali; you are so kind. Perhaps you could contact me later, if you have any news. Goodbye."

Mary hung up and sat dejectedly on the side of the bed.

"Oh, Rose, what am I to do? First it was Huw, but now it looks as if his father Mike, is missing, too. Can it possibly get any worse?"

Chapter 6

Ahmed Investigates

"I am leaving for the fortress now, Abu," whispered Ahmed, "but this time I must go alone. I want you to stay here and guard Sheba while I am away. I shall return soon, at first light."

Abu whimpered as Ahmed crept quietly out of the black Bedouin tent in the early hours of the morning. He had only managed a few hours of restless sleep, thinking about the truck pulling the horse box high into the Hajar Mountains.

The night was eerily silent now that the sandstorm had blown itself out. The sky was clear and the stars shone like diamonds in the black desert sky. He felt as though he could touch them if he stood on tip-toe and reached high above his head.

He knew the foothills well, and a full moon enabled him to pick his way swiftly through the scrub and across the stone scree that lay in vast aprons at the feet of the vertical crags above them. Ahmed was as agile and surefooted as a mountain goat. It is said that Bedouin boys are born with this great skill, which is handed down from generation to generation. He wore a light cotton shift, which enabled his legs to move freely. His *farwa* kept him warm in the cool night air, and a loose turban wound over his long dark hair protected his head. His big, dark brown eyes glinted in the moonlight. He carried a short shepherd's staff, and wore leather sandals to protect his feet against the sharp stones and rocks. He wore a hand-carved leather belt around his waist, from which hung a goatskin water flask, a dagger, and a thin rope.

After two hours climbing, he had reached a height of 1,000 metres and he could see the dark, forbidding shape of the fortress outlined against the night sky. He moved carefully and silently between large rocks and boulders, using their shadows to conceal himself.

As he neared the fort, he lay flat on his stomach and wriggled his way forward. A sand lizard crossed his path, pausing to glance at him before moving on, unconcerned. He watched the guards carefully and moved only when it was safe to do so. Gradually, he drew close to the walls, and from a small opening at ground level he could hear the sound of a boy crying.

He crawled nearer to the opening, and heard the boy calling weakly for help and mumbling something about horses. The boy spoke in English, so Ahmed replied as best he could.

"Ssh, ssh," he whispered, "or guards will hear. I Ahmed, Bedouin boy. I go bring help. Come back when daylight goes. Stay calm and rest. You be O.K. Ahmed help."

The boy's moaning stopped, and Ahmed knew that he had understood.

"Before you leave," said the boy, "listen out for the horses; they need your help, too."

"Yes, I find horses," said Ahmed. "I know they also here in fortress. Not fear, I will be back soon. I have little water in flask.

I lower it down on rope. Sip a little through day. I back soon. Promise."

Huw looked up at the small window and saw a brown-skinned hand reach through and lower a round object dangling on the end of a thin rope. Its irregular shape caused it to twirl around as it swung down towards him. For a moment, Huw thought he was dreaming, and a cold shiver ran down his spine.He was feeling feverish and delirious. Who was this boy? Could he trust him? Was he real, or imaginary? He reached up and grasped the object with both hands. He realised then that this wasn't a dream. He could feel the cool, soft goatskin in his hands and drew comfort from it.

"Ahmed," whispered Huw, "you will come back, won't you? I don't won't to die in this awful place."

"Ahmed promise to come back. Bedou never break promise. Are you cold?"

"Yes, very."

"I drop *farwa* you now. Sheepskin coat. Keep you warm. Back soon, promise."

The coat came down on the end of the thin rope and Huw struggled to reach it, with cold hands and bruised fingers. Then, he released the rope and watched it disappear through the open window. He wished that he was a spider and that he could crawl up the wall and escape through the window from his dark dungeon. Tears welled up again in his eyes, and he wondered what he was doing in this place. Why had he come here? He couldn't remember. His head hurt, and he felt faint again.

"Back soon. Promise. Go now."

Huw's heart lifted as the words of hope tumbled down to him

from the window. He wrapped the woollen *farwa* around him and felt warmth returning to his body. He fumbled with the stopper on the flask, eventually released it and took a drink of fresh water. Water given to him by a Bedouin boy. He thought it was the most wonderful water he had ever tasted, as it slipped like liquid silver down his throat. Water from the oasis of life. There was still a little hope in his heart. He had found a new friend.

Chapter 7

Huw Tries to Remember

Huw felt the scab of dried blood on his head. The wound hurt badly. But how did it get there? He screwed up his eyes and tried to concentrate. The smell of acrid smoke suddenly filled his nostrils. There was a raging fire, but where was it? The sound of frightened horses filled his ears, and the clattering of hooves and banging of stable doors. That was it, he thought, the stables. But which stables? He had brief flashes of running along dark corridors, down marble stairs and past water fountains. But that didn't make any sense. That wasn't home. Where was home? He had flashes of different faces, his mother's face, his father, Aunt Rachel, Arthur.

"Yes, Arthur," he called out. "Where are you, Arthur? You're never around when I need you."

His shouting brought the prison guard to investigate. Huw saw a small panel open in the large, iron door. A dark, swarthy face peered into the dimly lit cell. It was a hard face, leathery skinned, and around the mouth was a nest of black hair, dripping with foul smelling food remains and liquid. The man's teeth were black and rotten, and Huw could smell his evil breath contaminating the cell. He felt nauseous again, and his head was swimming.

"What's wrong with you?" growled the face. "I'll bring you food and water, when I have finished eating. Just shut up, or I'll bring the whip to you."

The man thrust his one eye right up against the opening, and glared at Huw. It was a dark eye, like a black hole. It reflected no light or colour; a bottomless pit, a cavern, one empty void, a cold icy pool. Huw shrank away from it, and prayed it would go away.

The black eye disappeared from the hole in the door, and the guard slammed the iron panel shut. The cell reverberated with the vibrations from the door, and the cold metallic sounds jarred on Huw's fragile senses. He shook violently for a few minutes. He was filled with a mixture of fear, uncertainty and despair. His body temperature raged from hot to cold. But through all the pain and suffering, there was a ray of hope.

"Ahmed," he whispered as he pulled the *farwa* around him tightly, its warmth bringing him a feeling of security in this dark cell. He curled his fingers around the smooth goatskin of the flask. He could feel the cool liquid moving like mercury as he squeezed the flask gently. It reminded him of squeezing a rubber ball. It felt good to mould the liquid in his palms.

"Ahmed," he repeated, "you will come back, won't you? You promised."

The iron door swung open and clanged loudly against the wall. The guard entered the cell. He was clothed in black from head to foot, and reminded Huw of Darth Vader, except that he didn't have a black helmet. His head was swathed in a large, black turban; layers of cloth wound round and round his head, which made it look twice its normal size. His dirty face was bursting with hair. Heavy brows, big moustache, straggly beard still dripping with food. He glowered at Huw, but luckily did not notice the coat which Huw held tightly around him, or the flask hidden beneath.

"Here's some food and water for you, brat," the guard muttered harshly. "That's all you'll get today. You should keep your nose out of other people's business."

He swung around sharply and left the cell, taking his foul smells with him. Huw breathed a huge sigh of relief, and took a long cool drink from the water in the flask. The water Ahmed had given him, not the brackish water in the tin cup, which the guard had left along with a stale crust of bread. The flask contained fresh water from the oasis near the Bedouin encampment. This was, to Huw, the fountain of life and hope. Something magical in the water told him that Ahmed would come back when darkness fell. He knew he would, he could feel it in his bones!

Chapter 8

Henry Takes Charge

Dawn was breaking as they huddled together in the back of an ambulance. Arthur, Shakra and Nasra were draped in blankets, sipping hot drinks, and receiving medical treatment for their minor cuts and bruises. It had taken the emergency services all night to bring the fire under control; and half the stable block had been burned to the ground. All the horses were loose; they had galloped off into the desert, and would have to be rounded up later. Amahl and Henry were outside, talking to the fire-fighters and paramedics.

"I'm totally bushed," said Arthur, his face grey and covered with soot particles from the fire.

"Me, too," said Shakra, his wet hair dangling over his face and shoulders like limp tentacles.

Nasra sat with his head in his hands.

Arthur was aching more inside than out, as he thought about Huw and what might have happened to him. He had seen no sign of him in the burning stables, but the heat was so intense, and the choking black smoke had driven him back. Arthur wasn't normally given to tears, but he could feel his eyes filling up.

"You did your very best," said Shakra, putting his arm around Arthur's shoulders. "No one could have done more."

Nasra nodded. "You were very brave to go in there; do not blame yourself."

Henry climbed into the back of the ambulance. "There is nothing more we can do here now," he said. "The fire officers will remain here, to ensure everything is safe, and the medical team think it is best if we all return to the Palace. Two medical officers will accompany us. Come on Arthur, let's go and find Mary and Sam."

"But what are we going to tell them about Huw?"

"We'll talk about that on the way over. Come on, look sharp."

* * *

Within minutes, they were back in the safety and warmth of the large Palace kitchens. Sam and her mother Mary were already there, and the kitchen staff, Lily, Daisy and Rose, were busy making breakfast. It was soon a hive of activity.

"That smells good," said Arthur as one of the paramedics cleaned the dust and soot from his face and bathed his cuts and bruises. The warm kitchen was filled with the smell of freshly baked bread and the aroma of ground coffee. The large table in the centre of the kitchen was soon surrounded by tired and hungry fire-fighters, medical staff, Arthur and Henry too. To begin with, no one spoke, as they concentrated on eating and drinking.

But Sam was unable to contain herself any longer. "Arthur,

please tell us what you found. Have you any good news for us?"

"Afraid not," said Arthur, his face gaunt and tired. "There's no sign of either Huw or Ivory, and at least half of the stable block has been burned down."

There were gasps of horror from everyone sitting around the table, and Mary tried to comfort Sam as she burst into tears.

"I have more bad news," said Mary. "Mike is missing, too. He never arrived at the racecourse."

Just when everyone seemed to be in the depths of despair, Henry took charge. Henry Grant was a Squadron Leader and was used to taking over in emergencies. He was Sam's new stepfather, having married Mary Grant, Sam's mother, when the evil Dermot Kervlan had been killed by the wild boar in the ancient burial mound. Henry was also William Grant's brother; William was Sam's natural father.

"I know things look bad," said Henry, "but we mustn't lose hope. It's possible that Mary's horse, Ivory, broke free and stampeded with the rest of the horses into the desert."

"But what about Huw?" cried Sam. "There's no sign of him anywhere, unless ..."

"No Sam, don't let's think the worst about Huw or Ivory, until the fire has cooled and we've had a chance to search the stables thoroughly and rounded up the horses that escaped."

Everyone around the table nodded in agreement, and Sam felt her mother's arm tighten around her shoulder.

Then Henry turned to Arthur and Sam, and suggested that they go to their bedrooms and rest, whilst the fire-fighters and paramedics returned to the smouldering stables and attended to the injured guards in the Palace grounds.

"Mary dear, if you would accompany Sam to her room, I will go and find Amahl, Sheikh Rashid's personal bodyguard and emissary, and arrange a meeting with the Sheikh a.s.a.p. Then, I will ask Shakra or Nasra to drive me to the racecourse, to see if there is any news of Mike."

"Take care, Henry," said Mary, as everyone began to leave the kitchen. "Be on your guard outside the Palace walls; we don't know yet who's out there."

"Not worry, Ma'am," said Shakra, with a beaming smile, "Nasra and I take care of Mister Henry husband. We back soon. *Salaam Alaikum* – peace be with you."

Chapter 9

Ahmed Returns
to the Fortress

When darkness fell once more, Ahmed set off from the Bedouin encampment, but this time he had a companion.

"Move as quietly as possible," Ahmed said to his sister, in their native Arabic language. But he really had no need to say this; she was as sure-footed as he was on the mountainside. Like Ahmed, Sheba was clothed entirely in black, and the only sound she made was the gentle rustle of her *abaya* (cloak) as she floated along. Ahmed had asked Sheba to accompany him on this dangerous mission, as he needed help to carry food and water for Huw. This time, he also carried a larger and thicker rope.

After several hours of climbing the rocky mountainside, they were near the fortress. Sheba had not seen it this closely before, only from afar. Its angry outline and solid black mass looked forbidding against the night sky, and the moonlight cast threatening fingers of shadow towards them.

"Don't be afraid," whispered Ahmed, "but stay close behind me and melt into the shadows."

Ahmed waited until he was sure the way ahead was clear, and then guided Sheba towards the small hole at ground level, which acted as the only window in Huw's dungeon. They both crouched low and peered into the dark hole.

Ahmed cupped his hands over his mouth and whispered into the darkness. "It is Ahmed. I return with food and water. Are you O.K?"

"Yes," said Huw weakly. "I am so glad you came back."

"Ahmed always keep word. Now, I lower food and water to you on rope."

Sheba had secured a small basket to the end of the rope, and Ahmed lowered it down into the dark cell. Huw watched it swing to and fro, until he was able to catch it. His heart missed a beat when he saw the fresh dates and figs inside. He was so hungry, that he began to eat some immediately; they were so plump and juicy. He soon began to feel stronger, and as he ate he saw the rope descending once more, with fresh water in two goatskin bottles. He drank greedily this time, because he was so thirsty, and there was more water to save.

Huw thought he heard another voice, and at first thought he was imagining it. But then Ahmed explained that he had brought his sister Sheba along. Her voice sounded so comforting, but all Huw could see were two dark shapes near the window.

"Hello, Sheba," he whispered. "I wish I could see you more clearly, but there is so little light in here. It is such a terrible place ... you have no ..." Huw began to cry as the horror of his imprisonment gripped his mind once again.

"Not cry, please," said Sheba. "We will find way to free you. El Sufi will know way."

"Who is El S... ?" asked Huw.

"He our Leader," said Ahmed. "Once imprisoned here himself. Will know way out. Stay calm and rest. We come back tomorrow night."

As Huw looked up at the small window, a hand gave a brief wave, and then the two dark shapes disappeared. The silence closed in once more, but he now had hope in his heart. He lay on the rush mat which formed his bed. Although still weak, he felt better than he had since his captors had thrown him into his cell. The fresh water and fruit had given him strength, and he slept a less troubled sleep that night, thanks to the courage and determination of his two new friends. He hoped he would soon be able to see their faces and hold their hands.

Chapter 10

The Woman
on the White Horse

There had been something very comforting in Sheba's voice. It was warm and husky, and stirred his feelings deep inside. He had barely understood anything she had said to him in her broken English, but he knew deep down that she cared, and that was so important to him in his moments of unbearable despair.

In his deeper sleep, he had slipped for a short while into a very vivid dream. In his dream, he was sitting on a mound at the edge of an oasis in the red desert, when suddenly a woman came riding past on a beautiful white horse. The mare was tall, about ten hands high, graceful in appearance and yet full of power in her limbs. The woman wore a hood and cloak of gold, which billowed in the wind as the horse cantered by. She turned her head towards Huw and smiled gently with her eyes. Something in her smile drew him to his feet, and he began to follow the horse as it picked up speed. But, however fast he ran, he could not catch up, and he soon became breathless and had to stop. He returned to the oasis and lay down in the shade beneath the palm trees. Something told him that he must try to find a way to speak to this mysterious woman on the white horse, and he tried to think of a plan as the sun set over the red desert and the palm trees cast their long shadows over the shimmering waters of the oasis.

When the next day dawned, Huw once again sat on the mound at the edge of the oasis. He didn't have to wait long before the beautiful woman in the golden cloak came riding by. This time, she smiled and also waved. She seemed to be inviting him to follow, and now he was more than ready. He put his plan into action immediately. He leapt onto the back of the horse he had borrowed from the Bedouin people, who were camped by the oasis. The Arab horse was strong and fleet-footed, and well used to galloping on sand. Within seconds, he had almost caught up with the white horse, and his heart filled with joy as he opened his mouth to speak to the woman rider. But then, in an instant, the white horse pulled away at amazing speed, and there was nothing he could do to catch up, however much he tried to urge his mount forward. The only thing he could do was to shout.

"Please, wait," he cried. "I must speak to you. My life may depend on it!" His words floated away on the wind, far ahead of him, and much faster than any horse could run. Then, as if by magic, the woman in gold heard them. She tugged on the reins, and the white horse came to a standstill. She turned towards Huw and pointed to the distant hills.

"Follow me to the distant mountains," she said, "and there you will see a tall pillar of silvery rock. Behind this rock you will find a large waterfall, and behind the waterfall is a wide ledge. Once there, we shall be able to talk."

This time, the woman on the white horse rode at a steady pace and Huw was able to keep up. As the mountains loomed larger, he could see the pillar of rock, pointing like a finger towards the sky. Hidden away behind the pillar was the waterfall, and he followed the woman on the white horse onto the wide ledge behind it.

For some reason he did not understand, he did not feel afraid, and the cool air behind the wall of water was very welcome after the heat of the desert. The woman dismounted and stood before him in the shadows. He waited for his eyes to grow accustomed to the darkness and then he too climbed down from his horse.

He moved closer to the woman, until he felt a restraining force holding him back, and he knew then that he could not touch her. Although she was veiled, Huw was able to recognize the woman's features. That was because he knew her so well. It was his mother. But his mother had died; he knew that too. So, how could this be possible? Tears rolled down his cheeks.

"I know you have wanted to talk to me for so long, and that's why I have come to you now," said his mother, Beth. "You can talk to me anytime you wish, in your mind and in your thoughts. But most of all, you must speak to me with your heart, and then I can hear you loud and clear and I can send you my replies, too."

"But why did you have to die," asked Huw plaintively, "when I needed you so much?"

"I had to do my duty as a policewoman," said Beth. "I didn't want to leave you or your Dad, but life can be so cruel sometimes."

"And people, too," said Huw, "like the ones who are holding me prisoner now."

"I know, but you must be strong. There's something I wanted to remind you about. Do you remember the golden medallion, which you found near home, at the ancient burial mound? Well, I think you are carrying it with you, because I can sense its powers."

Huw fumbled in his trouser pockets, and there it was, warm to his touch as he closed his hand around it. As he gripped it tightly, he felt a surge of energy passing through him.

"Did you know that it has magical powers?" asked Beth. "You must look deeply into it, and tell it who and what you want to see, and whom you want to talk to. That includes me too. But it will go well beyond that if you really believe in it and talk to it from your heart. Its powers are unlimited, but they will only work for good, and not for evil. I'm afraid I must go now, as my powers are weakening."

"No, no, please don't leave me Mum."

"I will always be with you ... but remember to look into the medallion ... you must remember ... remember ... remember!"

The image of the woman before him and of the white horse began to fade and gradually merged into the reflections cast by the light filtering through the falling water. He sank down onto his knees and wept, and once more felt empty and alone.

Chapter 11

Sheikh Rashid

The sheikh's personal bodyguard, Amahl led Henry up the winding, oyster-coloured, marble staircase to the first floor of the palace. This floor housed the private suite of rooms of the royal family. Huge portraits of the sheikh's royal ancestors hung on the walls of the long corridor. Between the portraits were tall, gold-framed mirrors, reflecting the bright light that entered through the large windows facing out into the inner courtyard below. All doors were guarded by royal footmen.

Henry gasped as Amahl led him into the inner sanctum of the royal palace. The floors were covered in richly coloured carpets, and huge chandeliers hung from the ceilings. Marble walls kept the rooms remarkably cool during the heat of the day.

"Your Royal Highness," said Henry, with a gracious bow, as Amahl introduced him to Sheikh Rashid, the ruler of Dubai. "It is a great honour to meet you Sir, but I'm afraid that the news I bring is very disturbing."

"Come and be seated, Squadron Leader," replied the Sheikh calmly, "and join me for some light refreshments."

Henry knew that he had to be patient, as protocol was regarded as so important, when meeting any member of the royal family. Henry sat in a high-backed chair upholstered in deep blue velvet, whilst Amahl moved towards the door, to allow two servants to enter. They were dark-skinned and dressed in white robes, and appeared to be of African origin. They placed their trays of coffee and sweetmeats on a gilded table before the Sheikh, and then proceeded to pour the coffee from a *dallah*, a long-spouted jug, into small, white porcelain cups with gold rims. The servants left as quietly as they had come, and the Sheikh beckoned to Amahl to join them. He raised his cup and sipped the black coffee silently. Henry and Amahl did likewise. Henry knew that he had to wait for Sheikh Rashid to speak first, but trying not to stare, he cast quick glances at the Sheikh. He observed that he was short and lightly built, very handsome, with dark hair and a dark beard. He had sparkling, dark brown eyes.

"Well, now," said the Sheikh, smiling graciously at Henry, "what is this 'disturbing' news you bring. Does it have something to do with the fire at the stables? Amahl has briefed me, but I am not yet aware of the latest developments."

"Well, Your Highness, the fire has finally been extinguished and all those injured are being treated in the Royal Hospital. However, many horses have disappeared into the desert outside the Palace walls. We think some of them were released by those who broke into the stables last night. We think the fire might have been started deliberately, to act as a smokescreen while they made their escape."

"And what about the children? Amahl told me that they were the first to raise the alarm?"

"Yes Your Highness, that is true. It seems that Huw was first on the scene, but has since gone missing."

Sheikh Rashid rose to his feet, with a look of anger and alarm on his face.

"Gone missing? But how can that be? The security here is so tight. I don't understand any of this. Amahl, is this true?"

"Yes, Your Highness, by the time Arthur and Samantha had reached the scene of the fire, Huw was no longer to be found. Arthur risked his own life, by entering the burning stables to save the horses that were still trapped."

"Did he manage to get them out?"

"Yes, Your Highness."

"Allah be praised!" said the Sheikh, raising his arms skyward.

"But there is something else, Your Highness," said Henry, looking more serious.

"Something else?"

"When I spoke to Arthur this morning, he said he had been woken up, on the night of the fire, by the sound of a diesel engine, the sort you associate with a heavy truck. When he left his room, he looked through one of the high windows along the corridor, and saw in the light of the fire a large truck leaving the stable block."

"What!" cried Shiekh Rashid, his face now full of anger.

"And it was pulling a large horse box."

The Sheikh sank back into his chair as the full horror of what Henry had said began to sink in.

"Is there any sign of my champion horse, Ebony?"

Henry shook his head sadly. "I'm afraid not, Your Highness,

and it would appear that my wife's horse, Ivory, is missing too. They have not been recovered from the desert yet, and the only other alternative is ..."

"That they have been kidnapped," whispered the Sheikh, his eyes now filled with great sadness, "and, perhaps, the boy too!"

Chapter 12

The Trap Door

As soon as they returned to the Bedouin encampment at the oasis, Ahmed and Sheba went to see El Sufi. He was the oldest and wisest man in the tribe and was regarded as the tribal chief. His black goatskin tent was the largest in the camp, and he was always guarded day and night, looked after by his several wives.

Ahmed explained the urgency of the situation to one of the guards, who then disappeared inside the tent. He returned shortly and waved them inside.

El Sufi sat on a large, richly-embroidered cushion, smoking his *narghileh* (a hubble bubble pipe) For a moment he seemed to be in a trance. Then, his eyes opened slowly and he smiled gently at the sight of Ahmed and Sheba.

"*Salaam alaikum* (peace be with you)," said El Sufi.

"*Wa alaikum as salaam* (and upon you peace)," replied Ahmed and Sheba, in the traditional form of greeting.

"Please, rest yourselves upon the cushions my children, and tell me why you are here, and how I can help you?"

Ahmed began to tell what he had seen and heard over the

last few days, and how concerned he was for the imprisoned boy's wellbeing and safety. El Sufi's half-closed eyes opened wider and wider as Ahmed continued, and he puffed harder on his hubble bubble pipe.

"I know this fortress well," he said, "and the boy is indeed in great danger. I was once a prisoner there myself, and it is a difficult place to enter, or escape from. However, I found a way into the underground passages of the fortress, which will take you to the dungeons where the boy is a prisoner.'

"Then there is a secret way in," said Ahmed. "I prayed to Allah that there would be."

"Then, your prayers have been answered Ahmed," said El Sufi, through a cloud of smoke. Sheba coughed a little, but the wise old man didn't notice, or, at least, he didn't appear to. Sheba watched in wonder as smoke came out from El Sufi's nose and filtered through his brown-stained, white beard. He had a large beard, which, added to his turban, made his head seem much bigger than the normal size. His black, beady eyes peered through the smokescreen and fixed upon Ahmed and Sheba.

"I know what you must do," he said, "if you are willing."

Ahmed and Sheba nodded.

"You must first take some medicine to the sick boy. I will make this medicine immediately, from the herbal plants which I have in my store. This will help him to recover and regain his strength. Also, you must bathe his head wound with a liquid balm. While you are doing this, I will think of a plan to rescue the boy from the clutches of these evil men, whoever they are. But we must act quickly; there is no time to lose."

He rose and disappeared into the inner rooms of the large tent, and reappeared, minutes later, with a small, green bottle.

"Give the boy three drops of this medicine as soon as you can," he said, "and then tell him to repeat this dose again at night."

He took hold of a stick and drew a simple plan in the sand at their feet. He marked the fortress, and the position of the old stone well concealed by a mimosa tree.

"Memorize this," said El Sufi, "and then leave at once. Take great care, for these men are extremely dangerous. Tell the boy that we will come for him tomorrow, and he must not give up hope."

Ahmed and Sheba left the goat tent quickly, and set off once again for the fortress.

* * *

By now, they were well used to staying in the shadows and moving silently. They had no difficulty finding the mimosa tree, for it was much larger than any of the surrounding trees and scrub.

"You search one side, and I'll search the other," said Ahmed, "and make no sound."

Sheba nodded and crept quietly around to the far side of the tree. Although it was early spring, the foliage was already thick, following the winter rains, which fell frequently, high up in the Hajar Mountains. Sheba kept her head down and pushed her way through the dangling branches. For once, she was grateful for her head covering. Then she saw it, a low wall built of stone, with tangled roots and branches growing all over it.

"Ahmed," she whispered excitedly, "I've found the wall!"

Ahmed scrambled round the base of the tree, brushing aside

the branches, and there he saw it too. They pulled away the tangled roots, to reveal the stone steps leading down into the darkness inside the well. A dank smell rose to meet them.

"Come on," said Ahmed. "Follow close behind me, and be careful not to slip on the slimy steps."

They picked their way gingerly downwards, until they reached the bottom, where they stood in several inches of water. The water was bubbling beneath their feet, and they realized that there was an underground spring. Ahmed felt it was safe now to light an oil lamp, and soon they could see the arched roof of a stone tunnel stretching before them. The walls were wet and covered in moss, which gave the tunnel a musty smell. The tunnel was large enough for an adult to walk upright, so they had no difficulty in standing up straight. They followed the winding tunnel for some two hundred metres, until they came to another flight of steps ... this time, leading upwards. At the top there was a large stone slab, which looked as though it hadn't been moved in ages. Ahmed took out his dagger and started to scrape away the rotten mortar around the edges of the slab. He stopped frequently, to listen for any sounds from above, as he didn't want to alert the guard.

* * *

Huw woke suddenly from his deep sleep, the images from his dream of the woman and the white horse still vivid in his mind. He was suddenly startled by strange scraping sounds coming from the far corner of the dungeon. At first, he thought it might be a rat, but the sounds were somehow different ... more like ... but it couldn't be ... could it ... the sound of metal on stone?

He quietly removed the sheet which covered him, and crawled over in the direction of the sounds. When he reached the corner, he groped around in the darkness and felt the outline of a large flagstone beneath his hands. The scraping sounds seemed to be coming from right beneath the flagstone. He felt around for a loose stone, and tapped lightly four times on the slab ... dot, dot, dot, dash. The Morse code.

Ahmed heard the tapping and repeated the code on the underside of the flagstone.

Huw put his face close to the floor and whispered, "Is that you, Ahmed?"

"Ahmed come back," said a voice from below. "Please move to side. I now try to move stone." Huw moved aside and peered in the darkness as the stone began to move slowly upwards. Ahmed took the weight of the flagstone on his shoulders and heaved upwards, taking care not to make too much noise. Gradually, the stone moved upwards and then slid aside. Ahmed held the oil lamp up through the hole, and, for the first time, the two boys could see one another face to face. Ahmed saw the tears of joy glistening on Huw's face, and began to realize what an ordeal he had been through, since he was first imprisoned in the fortress.

"Everything OK now ... Ahmed and Sheba both here."

Huw grasped Ahmed's hand and pulled him through the opening and into the cell, and then they both pulled Sheba through. She was dressed all in black, and all Huw could see were two beautiful eyes, smiling at him through the narrow opening in the burqa. He had an overwhelming feeling of joy that he now had two friends to help him.

Ahmed wasted no time in explaining to Huw what El Sufi had

told them about the well leading to the underground tunnel. He explained about the medicine and gave Huw his first dose ... three drops in some cool, fresh water from the oasis. Then, Sheba helped Huw to some fresh bread and fruit, which she had brought with her, whilst Ahmed listened out for any sound of an approaching guard. So far so good, all was quiet outside the cell door.

When Huw had finished eating, Ahmed explained that El Sufi was working out a plan to rescue Huw from the fortress the following day, and it was important for him to take more medicine and food, to build up his strength. Huw nodded, to show that he understood, but he was still weak from his ordeal.

"You won't forget about the horses, will you?" pleaded Huw. "I cannot leave here without the horses."

"Ahmed not forget horses. Will explain to El Sufi ... He understand everything."

Ahmed reached out and touched Huw's face gently. "You not cry any more. We go now, but back soon. Ahmed always keep promise."

Huw smiled, and held out his hands to Ahmed and Sheba, before they lowered themselves back through the hole into the tunnel.

"You sleep well tonight after medicine," said Ahmed. "Very soon, tomorrow come, and you see sunshine again."

Then, they were gone, and the darkness once again began to close in on him.

Chapter 13

Medallion Magic

For a few moments, Huw peered down through the floor, and watched the light from the oil lamp casting long shadows behind Ahmed and Sheba, as they carefully descended the stone steps into the tunnel. He saw them turn and wave, and then the light grew dimmer and the shadows faded into the darkness. He slumped down by the opening and felt a fresh draught of air pulling through the tunnel. He closed his eyes and prayed that tomorrow would come quickly, and then he fell asleep.

* * *

He awoke at the break of dawn, as a cold grey light crept in through the small window.

"I'd better try to slide this slab back over the hole," said Huw to himself, "before the guard makes his early morning visit."

It wasn't easy, as he was still weak, but he moved it a little at a time, until it once more covered the hole. He scraped some of the old mortar back into the cracks, so that it wouldn't be too noticeable. Then, without thinking, he wiped his hands against his tracksuit bottom, and brushed against something. He plunged his hand into his pocket and pulled out the golden medallion. How could he have forgotten about it? It must have been the blow on the head, he thought, as a twinge of pain reminded him of his wound. What was it his mother had said to him in the dream? The medallion had magical properties: that was it, and that if he wished for something strongly enough he would be able to see it in the shimmering, golden surface of the medallion.

He moved quietly towards the outer wall of the dungeon, where the small, open window was situated. He stopped a few metres from the wall. The window was facing east, and as the sun began to rise, a shaft of sunlight pierced the darkness in the cell. Huw held the medallion so that the sun's rays lit up its surface. It gave off a dazzling aura of light, and the air tingled with the sun's energy. The cell was filled with a riot of rainbows, and it was as if the darkness had never existed. Despite the brilliance of the reflected light from the medallion's surface, Huw was still strangely able to gaze into its depths without hurting his eyes, and he was drawn by a powerful magnetic force into a time-tunnel. He began to see glimpses of his past, and he desperately wanted to remember what had happened before he was brought to this terrible place.

Images flashed before his eyes ... the monstrous yellow eye ... the ancient burial mound ... his cousin, Arthur ... and Sam ... his mother, Beth.

"No, No!" he cried out. He couldn't accept what had happened to her ... shot by terrorists ... he still didn't want to believe it.

His sudden outburst brought the guard scurrying along to

Huw's cell. He heard the keys being rammed into the lock, and the iron door creaked and groaned as it opened. The guard entered, looking haggard and dishevelled. He stank of stale food, booze and smoke.

"Now what's wrong? It's not time for breakfast yet, so shut up and stop whingeing." His voice echoed around the cell walls with the resonance of a Darth Vader sound-alike. His breath was foul. Although he definitely had Arab features, Huw wondered how he had such a good command of English. Perhaps he had spent some time in Britain.

"That's odd," said the grunge. "The air smells different in here."

He held up his oil lamp and peered into the shadows. Fortunately for Huw, his bloodshot eyes saw nothing, only blurred images which wouldn't stand still. He dragged a dirty sleeve across his eyes and grunted. He swayed for a moment and then turned to leave.

"Perhaps your cell is air-conditioned? Ha, Ha! What do you say, oh fair one? Ha, Ha!" He laughed loudly at his own pathetic attempt at a joke, and then slammed the iron door behind him. Huw breathed a huge sigh of relief as he caught sight of the loose dust and mortar around the stone slab in the far corner of the room. I'll have to be more careful in future, he thought to himself; no more shouting out, from now on; it's too risky. He gripped the medallion tightly, and stared once more into its depths. This time, he saw a picture of Ahmed and Sheba, as they made their way back along the tunnel.

He marvelled at the golden disc in his hand. It was just like having a Palmcorder with digital quality pictures. But he didn't have to press any buttons, just wish with all his heart to see something, past or present; and there it was, before his eyes. He no longer felt alone, but he knew he had to survive until tomorrow in this awful place.

Chapter 14

The Falcons

As Huw was discovering the magic qualities of the medallion, in his prison cell, outside the Palace walls, Colonel Kassim was supervising the early morning training sessions of the Royal Falconry Squadron. This was a special group of men, handpicked from the Dubai Royal Air Force for their skills in handling large birds of prey like the peregrine falcon.

For centuries Falconry had been very popular among Arab Sheiks and Emirs, and had lately become a firm favourite of Sheikh Rashid.

"Come on now, work those birds harder," barked the Colonel, "I want to see them rising to a greater height, and then diving at a faster speed."

Kassim was a tall, straight-backed, highly ranked officer, who commanded great respect amongst all the Sheik's military forces. He had dark, piercing eyes, brown, sun-tanned skin, and a flashing smile, when he chose to use it. His head was protected by a *ghutra*, a red and white check head garment, held in place with a circular black silk cord around his forehead.

Most of the falcons were brown in colour, with slate blue feathers on their heads and upper bodies, except for the leading falcon, whose name was Gyrid. Gyrid was all white with black spots on the wing tips and a strong black beak and talons. He was a magnificent bird, with a wingspan well over a metre wide.

"This time, Gyrid," said Kassim to the bird as he held him on his gloved hand, "I want you to go as high as you can, and then come down in a steep dive." Gyrid blinked at Kassim, as if to tell him that he understood. "If you see anything up there, then I want you to bring it down," said Kassim, with a twinkle in his eye.

Another blink from Gyrid, and then, as Kassim stretched out his arm, the falcon spread his enormous wings and launched himself into the air. The movement of the wings sent a powerful downdraught of air, causing sand to swirl around the Colonel. The take-off was an astonishing mixture of power and grace, and the bird gained height with remarkable speed. It was soon just a speck, high in the sky, as it soared upward on thermal currents of warm air.

"What's that?" called the Colonel, as he spotted something moving below the falcon. He steadied his powerful field binoculars and focused on the object. It was a carrier pigeon, heading for the palace walls. Several soldiers raised their falcons in readiness to strike, as no bird or flying object was allowed to pass undetected over the palace walls.

"No, wait," ordered Kassim. "Gyrid has spotted it, and has already gone into a steep dive!"

Large white falcons like Gyrid can travel up to 200 miles per hour in a steep dive, and he was just a white blur as he swooped on the unsuspecting pigeon and grabbed it in his large black claws.

Gyrid leaned backwards, as if applying brakes, and then opened his wings, to break the speed of his dive. He made a perfect landing on Kassim's hand. Although the pigeon was stunned by the hawk's impact in flight, he was not dead.

"I think he will live," said Colonel Kassim, as he released the bird from the falcon's powerful talons.

"Look," said Corporal Jabdah, one of Kassim's best officers, "there's a small note attached to the bird's leg!"

"So there is," said Kassim. "Let's see what it says."

The squadron gathered round closely to watch as the Colonel carefully removed the small piece of parchment, unrolled it and stared at it grimly. His long experience as a soldier in the Desert Corps and his rank as a senior officer automatically took over. He wanted to tell the squadron what the message said, but he knew it would be a serious breach of security if he did so. However, he also knew that his loyal band of men, who made up The Royal Falconry Squadron, deserved some explanation. He decided to compromise.

"I cannot tell you the exact content of the message," he said calmly. "However, it does concern the missing horses and the boy called Huw. That's all I can tell you at present, but you must be tight-lipped about this information. Not a word about this must pass beyond this place, and from your mouths. Any breach of security will have serious consequences. Do you all understand?"

The Colonel's gaze rested in turn upon the eyes of each man before him. They felt the steel in that look, and they knew that they had to remain silent. Each one bowed his head in agreement.

"Good," said the Colonel with a faint smile, "and now I must take the message quickly to Sheikh Rashid. Corporal Jabdah, I am leaving you in charge of the squadron."

"Yes, sir," said Jabdah.

"Please carry on with the training exercises until you have finished, and then return the birds to the Falconry as usual. I will meet you all there later."

Corporal Jabdah called out instructions to the men, as Colonel Kassim turned and began to run towards the Palace walls. He knew he must speak to the Sheikh at once. There was not a moment to lose. Many lives depended on it.

Chapter 15

Al Jackaal

After leaving Huw in his cell, Ahmed and Sheba had made their way along the tunnel towards the concealed entrance. Outside, they could hear voices, and realized that more guards had been posted around the fortress.

"Sheba, stay here in the tunnel and wait. I will go find out what is happening. Something is up," whispered Ahmed.

Sheba nodded, and crouched in the dark tunnel, pulling her cloak around her for warmth.

"I will be back soon, don't worry."

Ahmed emerged quietly through the tunnel entrance, and lay hidden in the bushes, until the extra guards wandered off. He then wriggled his way forward on his tummy, until he reached the base of the fortress wall. He moved soundlessly through the shadows, until he came to the west wall, on the opposite side. Above him there was a narrow slit in the wall, an 'open window' from which light shone above his head. He could hear voices inside, and one voice sounded more prominent than the others.

"Are the horses being well cared for?" boomed the strong voice.

"They must be well looked after if we are to receive a large sum of money from Sheikh Rashid and the British woman, Mrs Grant.'

"We are doing our best, Badrag," said a small voice.

"Shut up, you imbecile," roared the strong voice. "You have been told never to reveal names. Even here, in the fortress, we may be overheard. You are a stupid man, and will be punished now."

Ahmed heard the crack of a whip, and the small voice cried out in pain. There were several more cracks of the whip, and the small voice sobbed and whimpered.

"Take this man out of my sight and lock him in one of the dungeons to cool off. I will deal with him later."

A third voice asked the leader nervously what plans he had to spend the ransom money, if all went well. Much to the relief of the nervous voice, the strong voice roared with raucous laughter.

"Aha, Aha ... that's for me to know, and for you wonder about. All will be revealed when the time is right." His voice dropped and he continued with a hiss, "I have a great plan. I intend to avenge the death of my brother Hassan in Britain, and the deaths of other members of Al Jackaal throughout the world. I promise I will not fail you." He raised his fist and punched the air, shouting, "AL JACKAAL ... AL JACKAAL!"

"Al JACKAAL," shouted a chorus of voices. "Victory for AL JACKAAL! Together we will shake the world."

Ahmed had heard enough and he slipped quietly into the shadows, before the guards returned on their patrol. He found his way back to the tunnel entrance and concealed himself in the shrubbery beneath the mimosa tree. He waited to make sure that all was clear before descending the steps once more.

Sheba was so glad to see him, but she was beginning to shiver in the cold draught which blew through the tunnel. Ahmed wrapped his warm sheepskin coat around her and held her close until the shivering had stopped.

"We leave must here quickly!" said Ahmed. "There is much danger. I heard an evil voice tell some men of terrible plans. We must hurry back to warn El Sufi and the others right away. He will know how to help us."

They climbed the steps slowly and waited at the top, with bated breath. They could hear the guards' voices fading into the distance, and then they emerged from the shrubbery and began the long descent back to the safety of the oasis and the Bedouin encampment.

Chapter 16

The Young Woman
on the Black Horse

Huw struggled to take the medicine which he had been given. It had a bitter taste, but he knew that he must drink some every few hours if he was to break the fever which made him feel so ill. Ahmed had told him that it would help him to sleep and regain his strength. He began to feel drowsy and fell into a deep, dream-filled sleep. His head rolled from side to side, and his eyelids twitched frequently over his closed eyes. His breathing became uneven, and, from time to time, he had a spasm of shivering.

His dream became more vivid, and he saw a young woman approaching. She was riding a beautiful black stallion, and was covered from head to foot in a shining silver, satin cloak, which billowed out behind her. She stopped for a moment and turned towards him. He watched in awe as she slowly unwound the top of the satin garment from her head. He gasped, as he realized it was Sheba, and she looked so beautiful, dressed in silver satin.

"Come, Huw, it is time to leave this evil place. Mount up

behind me and I will take you to a safe haven, where you will soon be well again."

"But I can't move," pleaded Huw. "I feel so weak and I will never be able to mount your horse."

"Of course you will, just give me your hand."

Huw raised his arm weakly, but suddenly felt a surge of warmth and energy coursing through his body as she gripped his hand. He floated upwards until he sat behind her on the black horse. The satin garment wrapped itself around him until he felt as though he was in a cocoon.

"Put your arms around my waist," she said.

"I can't move them."

"Yes, you can; don't be so stubborn. How am I going to help you if you don't listen?"

"I'm so weak."

Sheba took his arms and pulled them around her waist. "Right, now hold tight; we've got a long ride ahead of us."

Huw was so drowsy that he hardly noticed as the ebony horse floated through the wall of the cell and set off through the desert towards the distant mountains. Huw let the weight of his body rest against Sheba's back and fell into an even deeper sleep. He felt as if he was floating above the clouds, and the warm sun touched the back of his neck. He could not feel or hear the drumming of the horse's hooves. But that was because the horse wasn't running on the ground!

As they reached the Purple Mountains, Sheba pointed upwards towards a dark cave, high amongst the rocky peaks overlooking a deep canyon.

"That's where we're going," she said.

"But, we can't go up there," wailed Huw.

"Oh yes, we can, but you must have faith, you must believe that we can do it." Of course, Sheba knew something that Huw didn't. He had been too busy sleeping to notice that Sheba's horse had been floating above the ground.

She leant forward and rubbed the horse's neck, and whispered something in his ear. He pricked up his ears, and nodded his head a few times as if he understood. Then she pulled lightly on the reins, and the horse rocked slowly back and forth before launching itself skywards. Huw clung on for dear life, but the horse soared high over the canyon and, within minutes, landed lightly at the mouth of the cave.

"I knew we could do it," said Sheba triumphantly.

"Why do you say we?" asked Huw.

"Because we couldn't have done it if you hadn't believed it too. Faith can move horses."

"Shouldn't that be mountains?" whispered Huw, still in a state of shock.

"That depends on who you put your faith in," replied Sheba, with a swirl, as she dismounted and then reached up to help Huw down. Huw wasn't quite sure that he understood exactly what she meant, at that moment, but it would have to wait until he felt stronger.

"Did you really know that the horse could fly?"

"Well, El Sufi has told me the story of the Ebony Horse many times, since I was a little girl, and I have always loved it."

"Isn't that one of the stories from the *Arabian Nights*?" asked Huw.

"Yes, it was one of the one thousand and one stories told by Scheherazade to the Shah, who had a wicked plan to marry as many young women as he could, and then have them beheaded the next morning. Scheherazade worked out a cunning plan to devise as many stories as she could, so that the Shah could never bring himself to order her execution. Each night, she refused to tell him the ending to each of the stories, so he had to wait until the next morning. El Sufi told me that if I really and truly believed in something, I could make it happen. So, you see, I did believe I could do it, and I had faith in you too!"

"You mean, you've never done this before?"

"That's right, never."

Huw felt a little faint, so Sheba steadied him, and led him gently into the secret cave.

Chapter 17

The Note

Colonel Kassim was perspiring profusely by the time he reached the Palace walls, despite the fact that it was still early morning and not yet really hot. As he approached the main gate he paused to catch his breath and straighten his uniform. Protocol was considered very important in all military matters relating to the palace and the royal family. Having composed himself after running hard, he saluted the guards as he passed through the gate, but he did not stop to speak to them, as he normally did. He marched across the courtyard at the double, entered the palace, and climbed the marble staircase to the first floor and the royal apartments.

He nodded to the security guards at the top of the staircase, and headed straight for the kitchens, where he knew he would find Amahl supervising the preparation of the Sheikh's breakfast. He was still a bit breathless when he spoke to Amahl.

"One of my falcons has just intercepted a note arriving by pigeon carrier. It is vitally important that I see Sheikh Rashid immediately."

"Of course, Colonel," said Amahl, quickly sensing from

Kassim's tone that the situation must be deadly serious. "Wait here just a moment, Colonel, and I will alert his Royal Highness to your presence."

He returned within seconds, and beckoned to Kassim to follow him into the inner sanctum. As he entered the huge drawing room, he saw Sheikh Rashid standing before a beautifully painted portrait of his beloved black Arab stallion, Ebony. He knew that revealing the contents of the note to him was going to be difficult, but he would not shirk his duty.

As the Sheikh turned to receive his loyal Commander, Kassim bowed deeply.

"Your Royal Highness, I have come immediately, to bring you this note, which we intercepted early this morning. Whilst it's not good news, I think it does provide us with a window of opportunity."

"Thank you, Kassim. Please be seated," said the Sheikh, as he took the note, opened a red leather case and placed his gold-rimmed reading glasses on the end of his nose.

Kassim could see that the Sheikh was deeply upset by what he read, and there were tears in his eyes.

"Your Highness," said Kassim, "if I might be permitted to speak."

The Sheikh nodded.

"This is clearly a ransom note, and those who kidnapped Ebony are demanding a high price for his life, and for Mrs Grant's horse too. But the good news is, Your Highness, that Ebony and Ivory must still be alive, and that if we can devise a clever strategy, then we might be able to outwit these criminals. I feel sure they would not harm the horses, because they know that they would never receive the ransom money if the horses were to die."

Sheikh Rashid smiled faintly. "You are a good man Kassim, and a very smart officer. It is at times like this when I realize just why you are my royal Commander. You are right; of course we must make plans, without delay, to secure the recovery of my beloved Ebony, and Ivory too. It would be unthinkable if they were to come to any great harm because we failed to take immediate action. As champions, they are irreplaceable. Who are these horrible men who would do such a thing?"

"As yet we do not know, Your Highness, but as we speak, our best intelligence officers are at work, and we hope to have an answer soon. Perhaps this ransom note will provide some clues. I will have it analysed as soon as I leave. We also have the carrier pigeon which brought the note. With your permission, Sir, I will call an emergency meeting this morning, so that we can devise a plan of action and a recovery strategy for the horses."

"Excellent, Colonel, and perhaps you would extend an invitation to Squadron Leader Henry Grant to attend the meeting. Let him see the ransom note, and allow him to inform Mrs Grant about the situation. I am sure she will want to know. But ask them to be discreet; we don't want any of this to leak out before we are ready."

"Yes, Your Highness, I will see to these matters right away."

Chapter 18

Ahmed tells Huw
about the Terrorist Plot

When he awoke from his dream-filled sleep, Huw was relieved to
see that Ahmed and Sheba had returned. They had brought him
fresh food and water once again, and Sheba knelt beside him and
cradled his head with her left arm while she bathed his face with
the cool, fresh water from the oasis. At first, he thought he was still
dreaming. If there was such a place as paradise, then this must be
it.

"Have some good news and bad," said Ahmed. "Which you
want first?"

"Better hear the bad news first," groaned Huw, "then, perhaps,
we can end on a high note."

"OK, bad first. Last night, I overheard men talking inside
fortress. Man with small voice beaten with whip by man with big
voice for speaking name of leader. He called Badrag. He spoke of
his brother Hassan, who was imprisoned in Britain."

At the sound of the name, Huw had a flashback to the time
when he was hidden away in Kervlan Court, and had heard the voice

of his now dead stepfather calling out the names of the terrorists who were present: "You, Hassan; you, Abuki; you, Miklovich! How long have we all waited for this moment. Now the day of revenge is almost here!"

"Are my kidnappers part of the same group which came to Britain last year?"

"Yes, they part of terrorist group called Al Jackaal. I have heard El Sufi speak of them."

Huw felt his heart sink. "Then, they are not finished yet."

"No, not finished by long way. They have more plans to kill and to destroy."

"What about the horses?"

"They OK at moment. This is good news. Kidnappers not hurt horses. They want big ransom money from Sheikh Rashid and Mrs Grant, before giving horses back."

Tears welled up in Huw's eyes.

"Second good news is El Sufi told me his plan last night to rescue you from this prison."

Huw's tears flowed freely. "Will it be soon?"

"Tomorrow," whispered Sheba, who had been largely quiet until now.

"Tomorrow," cried Huw.

"Sh ... Sh ... or you'll raise the guard." She held his hand, and his spirits soared.

"But, tomorrow," whispered Huw. "I just can't believe it. It's been so long. Quick, give me some more medicine, food and water. I must be strong enough to leave this place. Did he say when he would come?"

"He not reveal his plan till last moment," said Ahmed. "He say security better that way. No one must know what he plans to do, but he promise it will happen. He remarkable man with great powers. You have confidence. It will be O.K."

"Thank you both for all you have done. Without your help, I know I would die in this terrible place. But, before you go, there is something I would like to show you. I had completely forgotten about it following the bump on the head. But it came back to me in a vivid dream I had the other night."

"Must be medicine," grinned Ahmed.

"It's a gold medallion, which I brought with me when I came to Dubai. It once belonged to a nobleman, many centuries ago, in my homeland."

Ahmed and Sheba gasped as the light from the small window danced on its surface.

"This object has great powers," said Ahmed.

"How do you know that?"

"I feel it in bones, and know it is good omen. Have you ever tried rubbing it?"

"Why would I want to rub it?"

"Well, that's what Aladdin did with gold lamp he found. El Sufi tell me story many times."

"Well, I could try rubbing it, but, normally I just have to gaze into it and concentrate."

Huw couldn't bring himself to refuse Ahmed's request and so he rubbed the medallion with the tips of his fingers. As he did so, the ground trembled and Huw fell into a trance. He groaned and began to mumble something about a dream, in which he found himself in a dark cave, high up in the mountains.

Ahmed shook Huw until he came out of the trance.

"I know cave."

"What cave?" Huw looked startled.

"You go into trance after rubbing gold piece, and tell us of cave. I know cave you speak about. It high in mountains, near deep ravine. It called Cave of Magan."

"Or sometimes Copper Cave," said Sheba. "El Sufi told us many times of ancient cave dating from 3,000 BC, but very few people know how to find it."

"It excellent place to hide, when escape tomorrow."

Ahmed grinned widely, showing his brilliant white teeth, before going into a little celebratory jig.

Chapter 19

Reading the Clues

After receiving news of the ransom note from Colonel Kassim, Henry had gone straight to Mary and told her the news. Sam and Arthur were there too. Arthur was becoming restless, and nudged Sam with his elbow.

"I'm off for a walk in the Palace courtyard," he said, with a sly wink. "No good moping about here, waiting for more bad news. Got to do something. Wanna come along, Sam?"

Sam nodded and gathered up her things, ready to leave.

"Be careful," said Mary, "and don't wander outside the Palace walls. There may still be danger lurking out there."

"It's O.K. Mum, we won't do anything silly."

"Promise."

"Yes, I promise."

They left Mary and Henry discussing the ransom note, and ran down the great marble staircase and out into the courtyard. Members of the Palace guard were placed at strategic points, and eyed the youngsters warily as they walked past the fountains, in the direction of the burned out stable block. The stables were cordoned off, and parts of the wooden superstructure were still smouldering. As they approached the perimeter, an officer of the guard stepped forward.

"I am most sorry, but no one is allowed near the burned out stable block whilst forensic tests are being carried out. Also, there is much danger, as the ruins may collapse at any moment. Please do not step inside the roped area, for your own safety."

"We understand," replied Arthur, with a nod of his head.

The officer saluted them smartly and continued patrolling the area. They walked on, taking care to keep outside the cordon, until they reached the place where a heavy truck had left tyre marks in the sand.

"Arthur, look here," said Sam, pointing to the deep tread marks.

"Wow, look at the size of them!"

"Must have been a big truck, to leave marks like that."

"Yes, and look, there's fragments of stone and some patches of different coloured sand, too."

Sam bent down and began to examine the imprints, which formed zigzag ridges and channels running parallel to each other.

The officer kept an eye on them, but didn't interfere, as they were well outside the cordon.

"I think we'd better collect some of this debris and take it back to Mum," said Sam.

"Good idea, but before you disturb anything, let me take some shots of those tyre marks on my digital camera. Could you tell me when the guard is facing the other way?"

"Yes, but be quick."

Arthur dug his hand into his backpack and took out his camera. He got down on his knees and took a closer look.

"It should be possible to identify the vehicle from these tyre marks if I can get some close up shots with the zoom lens."

"Fire away now," said Sam. "He's talking to one of the other guards."

As soon as Arthur had finished, Sam began to pick up some of the debris which had been moulded into ridges by the treads of the tyres. She placed the samples into small plastic bags, which she always carried with her in her backpack. This was something her mother had taught her.

"All done," said Arthur.

"Yes, that just about does it."

"Right, let's get back to the palace and show your Mum and Henry what we've found."

They tried to look casual and waved to the officer as they sauntered back into the courtyard. But once out of sight they raced ahead, through the main doors, and up the marble staircase. Sam went in search of her Mum, and Arthur went to look for Henry, so that he could print his pictures.

Mary looked excitedly at the contents of Sam's plastic bags, and emptied them carefully onto a small table covered with a white linen cloth. She studied them meticulously, using a magnifying glass and a microscope.

"What do you think, Mum?" asked Sam eagerly.

"I think you did very well, Sam. I'm very proud of you."

"Does it really help?"

"Well, I'm pretty sure I know where this debris came from.

There are three different components here. Firstly, there's the dark coloured sand; secondly, there are the small pieces of grey shale; and thirdly, the small fragments of pottery." She wandered over to where she had hung a large map of Dubai on the wall, looked up at it for a moment, and turning to Sam said,

"Come over here and take a look at these mountains, the Hajar Mountains, and in particular, a place called Fujairah. There's an old fortress there, dating from 1790, but the foundations probably go back centuries earlier."

Just as Mary was explaining this to Sam, Arthur burst into the room, quickly followed by Henry. He was blustering.

"Look at these prints," he said excitedly, unable to contain himself. "Henry persuaded Amahl to let us use his digital printer and computer to download and print these photographs. Aren't they great?"

The prints had been enlarged so that the smallest details were visible.

"Amahl has gone to find Shakra and Nasra. He says that they know everything about all the various types of vehicle used in the desert areas, and we should be able to identify it from these prints."

"That's pretty impressive," said Sam, "but Mum thinks she knows exactly where the fragments left behind by the tyre treads came from, don't you Mum?"

Mary smiled and nodded. "I think this calls for a nice cup of tea. Don't you?"

"I think I'll call for Lily," said Henry. "A small celebration might be in order."

Chapter 20

Tracking the Kidnappers

Before Mary had finished brewing the tea, Amahl arrived with Shakra and Nasra. Amahl always kept himself in great shape, and he appeared to be breathing normally, whereas Shakra and Nasra were gasping from their exertions. Amahl had found them in the courtyard, washing their chauffeur cars, and bundled them into the palace, up the long staircases, along the endless corridors, and into the visitors' quarters.

"I ... so ... sorry ... Mrs Grant ... I... not. ... able ... speak ... no ... breath," stuttered Shakra.

Nasra said nothing as he was bent double trying to get some air into his lungs.

"Please don't worry," said Mary, trying to conceal a smile. "It's perfectly alright. Henry and Arthur, would you please bring chairs for our visitors, and whilst they are regaining their breath, Sam and I will finish making the tea. Then we can all settle down for a nice afternoon tea party. How does that sound?"

"S ... sounds w... wonderful," said Shakra and Nasra in unison, both bowing low in gratitude, and smiling broadly, showing their gleaming white teeth. Amahl stood straight-backed, with his arms folded, and glowered at the two chauffeurs. He was impatient to get on with the purpose of the meeting, and wasn't one for niceties.

Chairs were brought, and they all sat around the beautiful, gilt-edged, round table, which formed the centrepiece of Mary's dining room. Mary and Sam laid the table with delicate white porcelain decorated with bright yellow and gold flowers of the desert. Amahl looked nervously at Shakra and Nasra, who were normally given heavy mugs to drink from, in the kitchens. Mary brought in some Victoria sponge and chocolate sponge cakes, which she had baked that morning.

"We should do this more often," said Arthur, sitting on the edge of his chair, grinning, and waiting to be offered the first slice of cake.

"Behave yourself, Arthur," said Sam, with a gleam in her eye, "and, perhaps, if I cut the cakes, you would be kind enough to pass the slices to our guests first."

Arthur looked peeved, but nodded in agreement.

"Course I will. You know I wouldn't forget my manners at a time like this."

Amahl still looked on, with his arms folded, and straight-backed, but this time he was seated.

Henry helped Mary to pour the tea and pass the cups and saucers around, and when everyone had been served, Mary said,

"Well, now, let's have a lovely afternoon tea. Then, we can talk about important matters, but only after every last crumb of cake is eaten."

Everyone smiled and tucked into the delicious slices of cake.

Even Amahl unfolded his arms and took a big mouthful of chocolate sponge, which was something he didn't do very often. Shakra and Nasra were delighted to be treated as special guests, and they began to chatter away to everyone around the table. And so the ice was broken, and when everyone had more or less finished, Henry took control of the meeting.

"It seems that Arthur and Sam have unearthed, in a manner of speaking, some very important clues about the men who started the fire in the stables. But, there is something else I have to tell you, before we begin to examine the evidence which we have here. A few hours ago, I received a visit from Colonel Kassim, Master of the Royal Falconers. It appears that Sheikh Rashid has received a ransom note from those who set fire to the stables." There were incredulous gasps from everyone around the table. "It appears that they have kidnapped Ebony and Ivory, and are holding them to ransom. I have sent a message to Colonel Kassim, asking him if he could meet us here at 4.30 p.m." As Henry looked at his watch, there was a sharp knock on the door of the dining room. "That'll be him now," said Henry, "dead on time."

Henry opened the door and asked the Colonel to join them at the table. He wasted no time in asking the Colonel to update them.

"We are convinced that the ransom note is genuine, and at present, both horses are alive and well. However, it is imperative that we act quickly and devise a plan."

Mary interjected. "Before you go on, Colonel, may we show you some evidence which Sam and Arthur have discovered from tyre tracks they spotted just outside the perimeter of the burnt out stable block?" She placed the plastic bags containing the fragments on the table, and everyone could see that they were now fully labelled.

"I have thoroughly examined these fragments, and I am convinced that they come from an area in the Hajar Mountains near the old fortress of Fujairah."

Colonel Kassim studied the remains carefully, before speaking. "This is indeed very valuable evidence, and with your permission Mrs Grant, I would like to show them to my military advisers right away."

"Oh, and don't forget my photographs, too," chipped in Arthur, placing them on the table for everyone to see.

As soon as Shakra and Nasra saw the photos, they began to chatter away excitedly in Arabic.

"Ahem", said Amahl, clearing his throat. "Could you share your thoughts with us, if you please?"

"So ... sorry ... everyone," said Shakra. "We ... just got carried away."

"Yes ... carried ... away," said Nasra, who seemed to repeat everything Shakra said, just like an echo.

"We see tracks like this often," said Shakra. "Made by heavy, how you call them ... 4x4's, often used in desert and mountainous areas. They have very large tyres with powerful grip."

"With powerful grip," repeated Nasra.

"I also know what is colour of vehicle."

"You do?" said Colonel Kassim.

"Yes, it camouflaged," replied Shakra.

"Camouflaged," echoed Nasra.

"There is place in Dubai, where several of these trucks are

kept in small compound. I see them often when I pass through Al Gachard Industrial Estate, not far from Dubai International Airport. I noticed they all golden colour, which makes them difficult to see in desert landscape, and they all had, what you call it – a logi on the side."

"Logi," said Nasra.

"Logi?" asked Arthur. "Do you mean logo?"

"Yes, logo, that it!" realised Shakra.

"Logo," said Nasra.

"And what exactly was the Logo?" asked Colonel Kassim. "Can you remember it, Shakra?"

"Oh, yes. Not possible to forget. It Black Dog's Head."

Colonel Kassim stared wide eyed at Shakra.

"You and Nasra have given us very valuable information. I too have recently seen a truck bearing this logo, but it wasn't a black dog. It was a jackal. We have been unable so far to track it down. This is excellent news, and I will order my Special Desert Commando Force (SDCF) to visit this site immediately. Also, I am greatly indebted to Mr Arthur and Miss Sam, and to you, Mrs Grant, for your analysis of the fragments. Perhaps I could ask Squadron Leader Grant if he will accompany me to my headquarters at once, for a meeting with my group commanders, so that we can work out a plan of action in relation to the Fort Fujairah area."

"I will be honoured to accompany you," said Henry, "but can I advise a word of caution. The element of surprise will be most important, if the horses are to be saved. I am also of the opinion that Huw may also be in the hands of the kidnappers."

"Oh Henry, do you really think Huw is being held, too?" said Sam.

"I have had strong suspicions from the start, but there has been little evidence to show exactly what happened to him. We can only hope and pray that he is still alive and well."

"This is another reason why we must approach this matter with great caution," replied Colonel Kassim. Then he rose from his chair. "However, there is not a moment to lose. Come, Henry, we must inform Sheikh Rashid of our intentions, and mobilise our forces quickly, if we are to defeat these evil terrorists who call themselves Al Jackaal."

Chapter 21

El Sufi's visit to the Fortress

It was two hours before dawn was due to break, when El Sufi, Ahmed and Sheba left the Bedouin encampment under the cover of darkness. It was a cold, clear night, the sky filled with large, bright stars, glittering like jewels in the inky blackness of space. A new crescent moon gave them some light, but El Sufi carefully led them through the long shadows of the dunes, before they began the slow climb into the foothills of the Hajar Mountains. They each rode a separate camel, and there was a fourth camel, loaded with provisions and goat skins filled with El Sufi's mysterious liquid. They were all disguised, with El Sufi dressed as a very rich merchant, in red and gold silks and a white silk turban, but they were all cloaked in black for the journey.

They had made thorough plans, so that they could maintain silence for as long as possible. As they approached the fortress, daylight was breaking.

El Sufi called out to the guards on watch, "Wares for sale! Wares for sale! Wine, silks and spices from the Orient. Precious jewels! Come and see!"

"Stop where you are," shouted one of the guards, "or risk being killed. Wait there until one of my superiors can see who you are and inspect your wares. This fortress is forbidden territory to strangers, and it is unlikely that you will be admitted. Where are you from, merchant?"

"Why, from the East, of course. I have travelled from the Orient along the old Silk Road, through Samarkand and Tashkent, to reach the shores of Arabia. I have brought two young servants with me to help with the merchandise, as I am now quite old. I mean you no harm, but please allow me to show your Leader my wares. I promise you he will not be disappointed, and will reward you for your good judgement."

The guard called out to someone down below, inside the walls. Then voices could be heard; passing the message to and fro. Eventually, the Leader himself emerged, wearing an armband with the sign of a Jackal. He seemed far less suspicious than the guard, and showed no fear of the merchant and his two companions, who had now removed their cloaks and sat there in their fine silks and satins.

"I hear you have brought wine with you, merchant. We have had nothing but water for weeks now, and my men are craving some fine wine and sweetmeats."

"I can promise you the finest wines you have ever tasted, oh mighty one, and, not only that, but I also carry an elixir the likes of which you have never tasted before. The elixir of the gods!"

El Sufi ordered his camel to lower him to the ground. Then, he walked over to the loaded camel and removed two goatskins. He lifted one to his lips and took a long draught. Thenhe handed the Leader the other skin, which contained a mysterious liquid which he had spent all night concocting. The elixir.

The Leader was eager to try the elixir, and drank greedily from the goatskin. The liquid was silky smooth and deliciously sweet, with a touch of bitterness. El Sufi had used this ancient recipe before, in such situations as this, and he only used the finest ingredients, including red wine, honey, and a secret blend of herbs. Now, it so happened, that one of these herbs was a sleeping drug, but it worked very slowly on those who drank it, and at first it created a great sense of euphoria.

"Come into the courtyard," said the Leader, already feeling very pleased with himself. "You must be tired after your long journey. This is indeed a wonderful elixir, and I feel years younger already. Ha, ha! What a great day this is going to be. I can feel it in my bones!"

The Leader led them through the heavy wooden doors of the outer walls and into the courtyard. Once inside, they could see that there was an inner fortress, or keep, inside the outer walls, and this was very heavily guarded. The Leader appointed two of his men to help unload the dozens of goatskins from the fourth camel, and then invited the guards to join them for a drink. They were soon drinking heavily, being unable to resist the aromatic flavour of the wine. At first, they sang and danced merrily, as the elixir cast its spell upon them. But gradually, they began to keel over and fall into a deep sleep.

"The elixir is beginning to work," whispered El Sufi to Ahmed and Sheba.

"How long will they sleep?" asked Ahmed.

"Oh, for quite some time, but we will need to hurry if we are to find the horses. Let's pray to Allah that they are safe and well. I will go with Sheba into the keep, for I am sure that's where they will be, and perhaps you, Ahmed, would go and find the boy you call Huw. But first, we must find the keys. Come and help me search the guards."

* * *

They found the keys on the two guards who had been standing guard when they first arrived at the fort. El Sufi took the bunch marked 'Keep', whilst Ahmed kept the ones marked 'Outer walls and cells'.

"I'm sure you know where to search for your friend Ahmed, but hurry, as there is much to do before we can make an escape from this place."

Ahmed nodded and made for the outer walls on the far side of the fort. El Sufi and Sheba went straight to the keep and began trying out the keys, until they found the one which opened the heavy wooden doors. They heaved against them until there was just enough room to squeeze through, and then found themselves in an inner courtyard, with a high stone tower in the centre. It was high enough to stand above all the other walls, and formed a central look-out.

"Listen El Sufi," said Sheba, "I can hear the sound of the horses moving. You were right; they ARE locked up inside the tower."

"Find the key quickly; we must get them out without delay."

Sheba worked deftly with her nimble fingers and, within seconds, she had opened the tower door. Moments later, they stood before two of the most magnificent horses they had ever seen. One was Ebony and the other Ivory. Both El Sufi and Sheba were used to working with animals, and they moved silently towards them, touching them gently, breathing into their nostrils and whispering to them. The horses knew instinctively that they were friends, and had not come to harm them. They stood quite still while their restraining ropes were removed, and then followed their rescuers out of the dark tower and into the bright sunlight.

* * *

Ahmed's thoughts were totally focused on Huw. It did not take him long to locate the door leading to the cells beneath the outer walls. He followed a winding stone staircase that led to a labyrinth of corridors. There were dozens of cells, but only one cell door was locked, the one at the far end of the corridor. As Ahmed raced towards, it he could hear a familiar voice calling out.

"Is that you, Ahmed?" The voice was weak and pitiful.

"It me. I coming fetch you now."

He rattled the key in the lock of the great iron door, unlocked it and then heaved against it with all his might. It creaked and groaned as it opened slowly, and a moment later he stood face to face with Huw.

"Ahmed here. I promise you I come."

Huw was in tears, and his body shook with emotion at the thought of being freed. They hugged one another like long lost brothers. It was a moment neither of them would ever forget.

"It OK now. No more cry. I take you meet El Sufi and Sheba. They go look for horses."

Ahmed supported Huw as they made their way along the dark corridor, up the stone staircase and into the bright sunlight. Huw shielded his eyes, and was temporarily blinded by the bright light. Gradually, they made their way around the central tower, and then they saw the horses. Huw's heart leapt with joy; Sheba ran towards him and hugged him too. Then, he stood face to face with El Sufi, the wise old man about whom he had heard so much. As he looked into his eyes, he felt an enormous sense of peace. It was as if they contained all the wisdom and knowledge of eternity. But, even more than that, they were full of compassion. No words were spoken at that moment, but Huw felt that the old man could read his innermost thoughts and knew what pain he had endured. El Sufi reached out and took Huw's hands in his own. As they touched, Huw felt a strong force of energy pass through his body, rejuvenating his mind and spirit.

"We will talk later, my son, for we have much to talk about. But now we must hurry if we are to reach the secret cave in safety. Ahmed, help Huw onto your camel, and then mount up yourself. You will need to support him as he is still very weak. Sheba, you mount up too, and look after the camel carrying the provisions. I will scatter the terrorists' horses and puncture the tyres in their trucks, to slow them down as much as possible. Then I will lock the doors in the outer walls and throw away the keys."

"What about Ebony and Ivory?" croaked Huw.

"Fear not, my son. I will take their reins and lead them after me. Trust me, all will be well. Now, let's be off if we are to reach the secret cave before nightfall. It's a long ride."

They all felt a great sense of relief, as they left the fortress behind them and rode higher into the mountains. The fortress grew smaller and smaller until it was no more than a dot on the horizon. But would they make it to safety? Al Jackaal was a formidable force to be reckoned with.

Chapter 22

The Pursuit

"Now, gentlemen, the time has come for action."

Colonel Kassim sat at the head of a long rectangular table, with all his most Senior Commanders. Henry sat on his right, and Sheikh Rashid's personal secretary was on his left, to take minutes of the meeting.

"I would like to know what you consider are the best possible options for approaching the fortress, bearing in mind that we must save the horses and young Huw, who is almost certainly imprisoned there, too."

A Senior Commander from the Desert Corps rose to his feet.

"I suggest Colonel, that we consider a Special Forces Unit (SFU) raid after dark; these Forces are highly trained to approach by stealth."

"We could also create a diversion or two by moving troops into other areas, to convince the kidnappers that we are not on their scent," said a second Commander, "and perhaps a fire could be started in the scrubland, a few miles away."

Henry asked Colonel Kassim for permission to speak. "May

I suggest broadcasting a message on radio, which should reach the kidnappers, saying that Sheikh Rashid is prepared to pay the ransom and is organising a special envoy to take the ransom to a place acceptable to the leader of the Group?"

"That's an excellent idea," said Kassim. "I will arrange for you to speak with Sheikh Rashid immediately following this meeting. If he agrees, then he will appoint a suitable envoy to proceed with haste. While the envoy is making his way to the rendezvous, we will organize a night-time raid by the SFU to take place after the ransom money has been handed over. I do not trust these people, I fear they will not honour their word, and will kill the hostages afterwards."

Everyone at the table looked grimly around at one another, after Colonel Kassim's final words, for they knew from recent experiences that these men could not be trusted to keep their word and were only interested in receiving the rich ransom to further their evil plans.

Colonel Kassim rose to his feet, and all the officers present followed.

"Each of you knows what to do, we must all act quickly and secretly to mobilize our forces. Be ready to move by 8 p.m. this evening. Good luck, gentlemen, and may God be with you."

Each of the officers saluted as the Colonel, Henry, and the Secretary left the room. But, at this time, they had no way of knowing that El Sufi, Ahmed, Sheba and Huw were already leaving the fortress and heading for the secret cave.

* * *

Badrag shook his head violently to and fro as he began to recover from the effects of the sleeping drug. At first, he could not remember what had happened. He looked around the fortress and saw his men scattered everywhere, lying where they had fallen, still clutching their goatskins.

"Goatskins, goatskins," he repeated several times. "Why are they holding goatskins?"

Then, gradually, he began to recall what had happened several hours earlier ... the arrival of the rich merchant, his helpers, the camels, the elixir ..."THE ELIXIR!" he shouted. "That's what it was, that wily old merchant must have drugged the elixir!"

He hauled himself to his feet and staggered across the inner courtyard, kicking anything in his path, including the sleeping guards.

"Wake up, wake up," he yelled. "For the love of Allah wake up. We have been duped; the merchant has out-witted us, and ... and —" His eyes fell upon the open door to the Tower and the horses hoof-prints in the sand. "The horses ... the horses ... they've taken the horses. Wake up you scum, help me to search for them."

Some of the bedraggled guards staggered to their feet, looking much the worse for wear after guzzling gallons of the deliciously sweet elixir. They could scarcely keep their eyes open, but they tried to appear willing, or they would be viciously whipped by Badrag.

It soon became clear to Badrag that the horses were gone. He lurched towards the prison door, and practically fell down the steps leading to the dungeon in which Huw had been held prisoner. The prison guards were still asleep, the prison door ajar, and he knew the worst. Huw was gone too. He slammed the door shut, and kicked the guards on the floor.

"Wake up, you fools; can't you see they've deceived us? Isn't there anyone here I can trust to do their job? You're all idiots, idiots!"

The guards stirred, under the constant tirade from Badrag.

"Follow me you dogs, and help me raise the alarm. I want all my men aroused and ready to move in 30 minutes – do you understand – 30 minutes!"

The prison guards fell about, trying to regain their balance and climb what seemed like a moving staircase 1,000 steps high, although it was only thirty. They gasped and wheezed as they tried to draw air in through their dry and constricted throats, which were still partially paralysed from the effects of the elixir.

"Yes, Leader," they croaked, "we are coming, we are coming."

Half an hour later, all the men were assembled in the inner courtyard. Without exception, they all looked the worse for wear, their hair dishevelled, their clothes hanging loose. Their eyes were sunken into deep hollows, which looked like miniature black holes. As they looked up at their Leader, all they could see was a line of swirling light, as if they were looking down on to a spinning top. Only one or two had managed to recover their horses, so they were far from ready for action.

"I am going to lead a group of my best men in pursuit of the merchant and the others," he shouted at the half-interested crowd before him. "I will leave Agra Vata, 'The Hook', in charge of the remainder, to guard the fortress and to await the arrival of the envoy with the ransom."

He turned to face The Hook. "I am relying on you to do your duty here, Hook. You must not fail. Understand! Tell the Envoy that I have left to bring the horses from the place where they are being held. Whatever happens, you must not let him leave here with the ransom money. Do you understand?"

"Yes, Leader, I understand and I will not fail you." The Hook trembled inside, for he knew what would happen if he failed.

"Good, then let us begin the pursuit of these thieves. The merchant and his helpers will pay for this with their heads, as will anyone of you who fails to do his duty."

Chapter 23

Inside the Secret Cave

After what seemed like hours of climbing high into the Hajar Mountains, Huw felt waves of weariness sweeping over him. Only Ahmed's strong arms prevented him from collapsing and falling from the camel.

"Hold on Huw, we're almost there now," whispered Ahmed, "then you be safe to rest and sleep deeply."

Darkness was closing in, and the night air felt colder and sharper as they continued to climb. Patches of snow were now visible in the rocky crags, and they reflected an eerie light onto the landscape, so that it seemed to transform itself into a black and white chessboard.

"Wait! Listen ... I hear something!" Ahmed's keen hearing had picked up a distant sound on the light breeze. "Horses ... many horses ... they are coming."

El Sufi pointed to the ridge high above them – and there they saw a clump of umbrella thorn trees. "Behind those acacia trees is the secret cave; we are almost there."

"But, there is a ravine between us and the cave," said Huw.

"How are we going to cross?"

"Do you remember the dream about the Black Horse?" said Sheba.

"Yes, yes," spluttered Huw, "but you can't mean fly ... but how?"

"Remember, you have to believe you can do it, Huw. You did it before, remember?"

"It can be done," said El Sufi. "Follow me, and I will show you the way." He rode his camel to the edge of the ravine, and then they suddenly rose above the ravine together with the horses.

Huw closed his eyes. He saw his Mum, his Dad and Sam too.

"I can do this. I know I can, I believe I can do it."

"You do it," said Ahmed. Ahmed's camel floated gently into the air above the ravine. It was as if they were being carried skywards by the rising currents of warmer air from the deep chasm below. Huw clung on tightly to the reins, and Ahmed's arms held him firmly.

They landed safely on a ledge near the umbrella trees, and followed El Sufi into the concealed entrance to the cave. A tunnel led into a large central chamber, which appeared to have a golden roof, which was reflected in a lake below.

"Welcome to the Cave of Magan ... Magan. ...Magan," said El Sufi, his voice echoing around the large dome. "It is sometimes known as the Copper Cave. It is very old and dates from 3,000 BC, the time of the Sumerians, who were the first people to work the copper in this cave. By mixing the copper with tin they learnt how to create beautiful bronze objects. We shall be safe here from our pursuers, as they will not be able to reach us for some time, if at all.

Now we must all eat, drink, rest, and then when we are refreshed, we can plan our next move."

Ahmed and Sheba tended to the camels, whilst Huw, determined to do his bit, watered and fed the horses. El Sufi prepared a nutritious meal, and soon afterwards, they were all soundly asleep. All except one. Ahmed sat near the entrance to the cave, to keep watch. They had agreed, during the meal, to take it in turns to stand guard.

Several hours passed quietly, and then Ahmed roused Sheba, to take the second watch. She took up her position out of sight behind the umbrella tree. Not long afterwards, she heard voices drifting upward from down below in the ravine. One voice was louder than the others, and he was obviously the leader. It was Badrag.

"We have searched the area widely, but there are no signs of them anywhere. It doesn't make sense. There are no tracks from the camels or the horses beyond the top of the ravine."

"Perhaps, they doubled back the other way." said a second voice.

"No, you fool, don't you remember, we followed the tracks from the fortress until we reached the high plateau, and then they just seemed to disappear, as if ... as if ..."

"As if, Leader?"

"As if they had gone underground. That's it ... they've gone inside the mountain somewhere, but where? I shall have to summon the forces of evil to seek them out. I shall call up the spirit of the desert *Djinn* (a Genie), Jackaala Dhobi; he will be able to see and smell exactly where they are."

"Jackaala Dhobi!" exclaimed the second voice in horror, "but isn't he the giant dust devil, the one who can whip the desert sands into the most terrible sandstorms and twisters, which in the past have wiped out entire nations of people?"

"Silence you wimp. Jackaala is our friend, and he will help us to find these infidels. They cannot hide from Badrag and the great desert Djinn. No one can hide from the Djinn. Ha, Ha. Ha, Ha. Ha, Ha!"

Sheba pulled back from her hiding place, and returned through the tunnel to find El Sufi. She could not wait; she had to warn him of Badrag's plan. She found El Sufi already awake, for the wise old man only ever slept for short periods at a time. He listened intently to Sheba's tale, and then said that they would have to waken the others to tell them of this grim news.

As they awoke, they huddled together on the edge of the lake, as it shimmered in the light of the early dawn filtering through tiny holes in the copper canopy of the dome.

"Sheba has brought me bad news," said El Sufi, and he explained what Sheba had heard. "I am trying to think of some way we can deal with this fearsome evil known as Jackaala, but nothing in my memory has so far pointed out the solution. I have never had to deal with this evil force before, although it has struck my people down in centuries past."

"I remember something," said Ahmed, "which might help. Huw has magic Medallion from ancient burial mound. He see things in Medallion, like mirror, and, also, if he rubs it like lamp of Aladdin."

As soon as El Sufi saw it, he knew that this golden disc was something very special. He could feel its force trembling in his fingers.

"It works best if there is light shining on surface," said Ahmed, "and look up there." He pointed to the fine pencil rays of light shining through the copper canopy, and beaming down on them like lasers.

El Sufi held the medallion so that a thin beam struck its surface. It glowed with immense power, and El Sufi could feel its enormous force surging through his body.

"Hold it Huw, and look into its energy field. You are the only one who can summon its life-saving force to our aid."

Huw clutched the medallion and once more gazed into its depths. The deeper he looked the more intense the heat became, until eventually he could feel the hot breath of the dragon.

"We need your help," cried Huw. "The forces of evil are being summoned by Badrag, and we will be overwhelmed unless you come quickly."

"Don't be afraid," said a voice from deep inside the Medallion, "I am Draco and I shall not let you down. You and I have met before, at the burial mound. But first, let El Sufi tell you about the powers and the weaknesses of the evil Djinn. He has something in his possession, which will help you."

The voice faded, and Huw looked at El Sufi, who was searching for something in one of his saddlebags.

"I had forgotten about this," said El Sufi, "but now your dragon spirit has reminded me of it."

He produced a small bronze spear. "This ancient spear is called Mar, and is believed to belong to the god Marduk. It has been handed down to me by generations of my forefathers. It was made to ward off evil spirits, and flies with the speed of lightning.

I will give this to you Huw, and you must hide it on your person, until you know the moment is right to use it. You have to strike in the mouth of the Djinn, so that it splits in two. This will return the world of chaos to its natural state:heaven and earth. But beware, because the Djinn can continually change its shape, and grow extra heads, so you will have to be sure which is the true mouth. There is only one way you can be certain of this. The true mouth will glow fluorescent green."

El Sufi's eyes moistened as he beheld his beloved Ahmed and Huw of the fair skin before him. He was deeply moved.

"This will not be easy for you, but when the time comes you must believe that you can do it, and that right is on your side. If you believe this, then you cannot miss. Now you had all better get some rest, as tomorrow as it is going to be a very difficult day. I will stand guard tonight, as I need to think out a plan of action for tomorrow. Sleep well!"

Chapter 24

Kassim Closes In

Whilst El Sufi was explaining to Huw about the special qualities of the bronze spear, Colonel Kassim and his senior officers were assembling their special units of the SFU. They were preparing for an attack by stealth on the fortress. All the troops were dressed in black, and could not be detected in darkness. Their weapons were also coloured black, so they would not reflect even the smallest amount of light. Nothing was left to chance.

Henry was, meanwhile, explaining to Sheikh Rashid the purpose of the radio and television broadcast. His special envoy Abrass Talib, was present too, along with Kara Mamzar, an experienced newsreader from DBC (the Dubai Broadcasting Corporation). Abrass was a former secret service agent belonging to a group known as DI9.

"I can arrange for the broadcast to go on air every hour, from noon today," said Kara. "That should ensure that the terrorists will pick it up."

"That's excellent," said the Sheikh, "then, my special envoy can leave during the afternoon, to take the ransom money to the fortress."

Abrass nodded.

"By the time he has arrived there, Kassim's forces will have left here under the cover of darkness, and will be ready to strike as soon as the order is given."

"Yes," said Henry, "and we also have plans to create diversions by setting off controlled explosions in various places around the fortress. Hopefully, this will draw some of their forces away from the fort itself."

Sheikh Rashid picked up a red leather attaché case which carried the Royal Ensign embossed on it in gold. He handed it to Abass.

"Guard this with your life, my friend, as it contains the ransom money, $100 million US dollars."

There were gasps around the table.

"You will have to go alone, but I know that you are well trained and above all, loyal, I have every faith in you. Remember that our special forces will be ready to move after dark, but you will have to use all your skills to delay them before handing over the money. Rehearse your story well."

"I fully understand, Your Highness, and you can be sure that I will not let you down," said Abass, who then bowed low, before departing.

* * *

The radio and television broadcasts began on time, at precisely 12 noon, Dubai time.

"We have just received an important announcement from the

Royal Palace," said the familiar voice of Kara Mamzar. "Sheikh Rashid has dispatched a special envoy to the Hajar Mountains. The exact location, and the purpose of the mission have not been disclosed, but we are monitoring the situation closely and will bring you hourly bulletins to update you with the news. It is thought that the mission may be connected with the recent fire at the Royal stables, and the kidnapping of two extremely valuable horses, which were in training for the World Championship to be held next week, on March 24th. One of the missing horses is believed to be the Sheikh's Arab stallion, Ebony.

"Also missing is a young British boy, Huw Pendry, who was a guest at the palace at the time of the fire. This is the end of this special bulletin. Tune in again, on the hour, every hour, for further news.

"This is Kara Mamzar broadcasting for the DBC in Dubai. Goodbye!"

* * *

It was 6pm when Abrass parked his distinctively coloured 4x4, with the Royal ensign fluttering on the bonnet, outside the main gates of the fortress. The terrorists were expecting him as they had monitored his progress every mile of the way. However, he had seen no sign of anyone until now.

A hooded guard came out to meet him, and escorted him silently into the fort. They entered the inner keep, where the guard led him to the quarters of the man left in charge by Badrag.

"Welcome, envoy," muttered the man, through a mouthful of blackened stumps, which were all that remained of his teeth.

"Are you the Leader of this group?" asked Abrass, from his dishevelled appearance and his shifty eyes Abrass could see this was not the main man. He did not have the bearing of a leader. Abrass was just playing for time.

"What does it matter?" spluttered the man, thumping the table with his right arm, which ended in a nasty-looking metal hook. "I have been left in charge," he yelled, raising his voice, and then cursing under his breath, when he realized he had said too much.

"It does matter a great deal to me," said Abrass, trying to stay cool. "I have been instructed by Sheikh Rashid to hand this ransom over to your Leader, and only after I have been reassured that the horses and the boy are all safe and well."

"Hand over the ransom now!"

"I will hand it over when you lead me to the captives. The attaché case is alarmed, and only I know how to disarm it. It will burst into flames if you attempt to force it open, and an alarm will ring in the palace, so the Sheikh will know that you have not kept your word and handed over the boy and the horses safely to me.

Sheikh Rashid is an honourable man and will keep his word. He expects you to do the same."

The man known as Hook was becoming more and more flustered, and began to realize that taking the ransom money from Abrass by force was not an option. He would have to think of a more cunning plan, but he was not a clever man, and this was soon evident to Abrass, who kept chatting away, much to the annoyance of the Hook.

"Will you shut up," he yelled, and thumped his hooked hand down on the table once more. The well-worn table shuddered under the impact, but Abrass sat there, completely unmoved. He noticed through a hole in the roof that darkness was falling and realised that Kassim's forces would be preparing for an assault on the fort.

Then, fate took a hand, or was it just good planning? Several loud explosions were heard in the courtyard, shattering the old wooden shutters, which were used to close up the open windows at night.

"Hook, Hook!" yelled one of the guards outside, "we're being attacked. Come quickly!"

As he spoke, a gas bomb exploded through the window. The Hook made a dash for the door, but it was too late. There, in the doorway, stood the towering figure of Colonel Kassim, wearing a gas mask. He threw a spare mask to Abrass, before grabbing Hook by the scruff of the neck.

"It's no use, Hook; it's all over now. The fort is surrounded and your men have been taken prisoner. Now, tell us exactly what's happened. I know you're not the Leader of these men, but at least you can tell us where the boy is being held captive, and also where the horses are being kept. You have ten seconds to tell us the truth or you are a dead man!"

The Hook fell to his knees, gasping and choking in the gas-filled air. He knew that he was doomed if he did not talk, and he was desperate for fresh air. He pointed to the open door, and coughed and spluttered until Kassim dragged him out into the open. As he slowly recovered, he began reluctantly to tell of the rich merchant's visit and how he had tricked them into drinking the elixir he had concocted for them. He told Kassim how they had awoken from a deep sleep, to discover that the horses and the boy had gone. In a fit of rage, their Leader, Badrag, had taken a small force of men and gone after them into the high mountains. That was as much as he knew.

Kassim acted with amazing speed. "Lock up this man with the others until I return," he barked to an officer standing behind him. He called another officer over and gave more commands.

"I want you to escort the envoy back to the palace, in complete safety. No harm must befall him, and remember, he is carrying the royal attaché case with the ransom money. Take a small troop of soldiers with you and proceed at once."

He then ran quickly across the outer courtyard, speaking into his mouthpiece as he ran.

"Kassim to base. Kassim to base. Send two Chinook helicopters to the old fortress at Fujairah, immediately. This is extremely urgent ... I repeat: urgent ...dispatch immediately. Over and out!"

Chapter 25

Flight to Freedom

An hour before dawn, El Sufi roused the children from their fitful sleep and told them he had prepared some breakfast for them. As they ate, he outlined the plan which he had carefully worked out during the night.

"Sheba and I will remain in the cave with the camels," he whispered. "Huw and Ahmed, I would like you to make your escape with the horses, just before first light. This should enable you to get past the guards, whist they are half asleep, and before they can raise the alarm. You will have to use the magic powers which I will bestow upon you, so that you can float down from the entrance to the cave without making any sound. You must touch down just beyond the far end of the gorge, and then ride westward until you reach the royal palace and freedom. However careful you are, you may still meet with resistance at some point, because Badrag will call on the powers of darkness to give him an advantage."

"What is he likely to do?" asked Huw.

"I have thought about that a great deal my son, and I think he is certain to call on the powers of the evil Djinn, Jackaala. You are a very brave boy. This I know already. But you will need every last drop of your courage and sharp senses if you are to outwit Badrag and his evil demon. However, you have a trusted friend, Ahmed, by your side and he will not let you down."

"I not let you down," repeated Ahmed, with a broad grin.

"You must also be ready to summon your guardian spirit, Draco, at a moment's notice, for only he will be able to match the power of the Djinn in a duel. I pray that the great God will go with you, and take you and these beautiful horses to safety."

"But El Sufi, I don't really want to leave you and Sheba here in the cave, at the mercy of Badrag's men," protested Huw.

"Fear not, young man, Sheba and I will be fine. I have magic powers too, you know, and I would never let any harm come to my beautiful granddaughter, Sheba."

Huw realized that El Sufi was not going to be deterred from his plan, and he reluctantly began to help Ahmed harness the horses. El Sufi breathed his magic breath into the horses' nostrils, whispered something in their ears, and then stood back and watched as Huw and Ahmed mounted. Sheba had muffled the horses' hooves so that they would make no sound when leaving the cave.

As the first faint streaks of light appeared in the Eastern sky, the two boys rode silently out from the cave and floated away in the crisp mountain air. They looked to Sheba like two majestic eagles leaving their eyrie. Their black cloaks spread out on either side of them like giant wings as they soared upward on the currents of air rising from the gorge below. All the guards were asleep, and it looked as though they were going to make a clean break. But there was one exception. Ravenna, Badrag's pet raven, was perched on the highest rocks at the end of the gorge, and with her sharp, bright, black eyes she spotted the two riders making their silent escape. She took flight immediately, and went to warn her master.

The raven soon reached her master's camp, and woke him with her harsh cry. Caw ... caw ... caw!

"What is it now, Ravenna, you stupid bird? Didn't I tell you to stay on guard at ...?" He turned his head to see the raven's eyes rolling wildly in her head, and he knew this was a sign that she had seen something and had come to warn him.

"What have you seen, my beauty?" His tone had changed dramatically. The raven lowered her head and pawed the sand with her claw.

"Horse!" shouted Badrag, rousing his men from their sleep.

Once again, the raven pawed the sand.

"Two horses," yelled Badrag. "Where?"

The raven lifted her wings and flew a short distance in the direction of the end of the gorge.

"They're escaping with the horses," he screamed. "She wants us to follow her! But how did they get past us here? It's the old man again; he must be a sorcerer. Yes, that's it; it's sorcery. Well, two can play at that game. It's time to call on Jackaala Dhobi!"

One of Badrag's men cried out in fear, "No! No, not Jackaala, please master! He is powerful, but his evil knows no boundaries. There's no telling what he might do. He might kill us all."

Badrag struck the speaker to the ground.

"Silence! I will decide what to do, and I am not afraid of Jackaala. Trust me; he is our only hope of recapturing the horses and taking the ransom money from the Sheikh and his allies."

The men fell silent and cowered in fear as Badrag went into

a trance and began to chant ancient Arabic words. He fell to his knees and picked up a handful of sand, which he then let trickle slowly through his fingers. As the sand grains fell he began to blow on them with his acrid breath. As they hit the ground, they began to turn in small eddies, to begin with, and then into larger swirls, until they grew into swirling columns of shifting sand.

"Dust Devils," cried the men. "We must seek shelter, for they will bring a great sandstorm."

They ran to hide beneath the rocks at the edge of the gorge, as the rising wind whipped the columns into larger twisters. They watched in awe as the dust devils plunged, wriggled, and swerved from side to side as if they were alive.

"Come out, you cowards!" raged Badrag, who had now come out of the trance but seemed totally demented. He looked up and saw the largest of the devils form a hideous head. It was the head of a monstrous Jackal, with the body of a lizard.

"Jackaala," he shouted above the roaring wind and the seething sand. "The horses are escaping. I need your help. Follow Ravenna and she will show you the way. Stop the horses from leaving the gorge, but do not harm them."

Jackaala spotted the raven and spun away in pursuit, followed by a huge swarm of dust devils. The whole gorge suddenly became filled with the roar of the sand devils as they blasted and scoured away everything in their path. Badrag followed behind like a raving madman, but his men remained hiding behind the rocks, in fear of their lives.

Chapter 26

The Evil Djinn
and a Swarm of Dust Devils

As Huw and Ahmed began their descent towards the entrance of the gorge, they saw what looked like the beginnings of a sandstorm blowing towards them.

"Is that a storm brewing, Ahmed?" asked Huw, as he clung on tightly to Ivory's reins.

"Strange looking storm," said Ahmed, "not natural. Very patchy, and something large bulging out front."

"Those patches look like whirlwinds."

"Yes, now I see better," said Ahmed. "They Dust Devils and the bulge is ... oh, no!"

"What is it, Ahmed?"

"Looks like monster El Sufi warned us about ... Jackaala!"

"The evil Djinn he warned us about? But I had no idea it would be so hideous."

"Yes, and remember that it can change shape. It may grow many heads and body shapes, to confuse us."

As they touched down they could see the sandstorm sweeping in towards them. The twisters were now merging to form an enormous wall of sand, which would be impossible to ride through, and it was so high, they would not be able to fly over it either.

"What are we going to do?" asked Huw.

"Take hold of medallion and call Draco, now!"

Huw nodded and rubbed the medallion vigorously before gazing into its depths. To his great relief, he saw the dragon's face.

"Come now, please Draco," he cried. "Jackaala has blocked our escape route with a wall of sand, and we can see no way out of the gorge!"

A dazzling beam of light shone forth from the medallion and filled the gorge with a ball of fire as hot as the sun. Then, the fireball formed itself into a dragon. It was Draco, and he had arrived at the speed of light.

Ahmed looked shocked, as he had never seen a dragon before.

"Don't be afraid," said Huw. "He is our friend, and will find a way of helping us if he can."

Even as Huw spoke, Draco sprang into action. He spread his wings and flew straight at the wall of sand. His neck was stretched full out and his eyes burned with fire. As he opened his mouth, an eruption of intense heat and flame exploded against the wall of sand. The heat was so intense that the grains of sand melted, to form a glass-sided tunnel. Draco flew relentlessly on, deepening the tunnel before him as he went forward.

"Come on," shouted Huw, "he wants us to follow him into the tunnel. It's the only way we'll get through the wall."

Ahmed looked terrified but he knew he must stay with Huw, whatever happened. The two horses flew as fast as they could into the mouth of the tunnel, and followed at a safe distance behind Draco. If they got too close the heat was too intense, and they would be burned to cinders. They pulled their cloaks over their heads as the dust was suffocating. Through the swirling dust, all they could see was a stream of fire searing its way through the wall ahead. The sides and roof of the tunnel were formed of crystal clear glass, through which they could see the swirling sand beyond.

"Look," shouted Huw. "There's something following us on the other side of the glass wall. It looks as if it's trying to break through the glass wall, but it can't. But I can't make out what it is."

"It's Jackaala," yelled Ahmed, "and it's changing shape to confuse us, also, to increase speed."

As they looked out through the tunnel wall, they saw the monster change into a large cheetah, and then into a jaguar, as it desperately tried to outrun Draco and the horses. It failed to establish a lead, even though it increased the number of its legs from four to sixteen, and eventually turned into a giant centipede with a hundred legs. This didn't work either. So then it became a huge serpent, with scales all over its body, to protect it from the driving sand.

Draco reached the outer wall of the sand barrier first, and burst forth into the bright sunlight of the early morning. Huw and Ahmed followed quickly behind, and were greatly relieved to be out of the suffocating atmosphere in the tunnel. Within seconds, the serpent broke through on their left, reared up like a cobra and spat poisonous venom into Draco's eyes, temporarily blinding him. Then it turned its hideous head towards the two boys, but now there wasn't one head but three.

"Not look into serpent's eyes," shouted Ahmed, "they mesmerize you. Look for real mouth; it glow green, like El Sufi say. When sure, strike with the Mar. It our only chance, until Draco recover."

Huw steadied himself on Ivory's back, and tried not to look at the monster's eyes, all six of them. He saw a brief glimpse of a green, luminous glow in the mouth of the head in the centre. He flexed his arm and threw the bronze spear with all his might deep into the monster's throat. At first, he thought that he had missed, as the creature came closer and closer. But then, it released a huge choking gasp. Two of the heads suddenly disappeared and the serpent changed back into the evil Djinn Jackaala.

Draco reared his head and cleared the deadly venom from his eyes. He roared his defiance at the Djinn, and breathed a sheet of fire at the monster. But this was no ordinary flame. It was a burst of blue flame like that from the exhaust of a powerful jet aero-engine, when a fighter plane takes to the sky. The noise was deafening, and the heat unbearable.

The boys watched in awe as the monster turned into a pile of smouldering blackened ash. The evil Djinn was no more. An eerie silence descended from the sky. The sandstorm was over, and there was no longer any wind blowing. The boys threw off their cloaks and dismounted, and walked without fear towards Draco, who was stretched out exhausted on the desert sand.

"Are you going to be alright?" asked Huw, with great concern.

"Fear not," said a voice which seemed to come from deep inside the dragon's throat. "I will rest for a few minutes, and then I will be well enough to return home."

"But you have done so much to save us; surely there must be some way we can repay you."

"I require no payment. My reward as a guardian spirit is that you and your new friends are safe, and that the evil Djinn is dead. The lives of the terrorists are now in the hands of the capable Colonel Kassim, and I am sure he will be victorious. Oh, and one other thing I should tell you is that Badrag will worry you no more."

"But won't he be waiting for you to leave before trying to recapture us?" asked Huw.

"You will have nothing to fear when I depart, because I have seen what happened when the evil Djinn died." Draco continued speaking in a deep, calming voice. "When Jackaala died, the sandstorm died with him, but, unfortunately for him, Badrag tried to follow us alone through the glass tunnel. However, he never reached the end of the tunnel, and now lies buried under hundreds of tons of sand. Alas, poor Badrag, I knew him well. Ahem, my apologies to Mr Shakespeare."

Huw grinned as he realized for the first time that even fearless dragons could have a great sense of humour.

"I hear engines approaching, so it time for me to take my leave. I wish you good luck for your return to the palace, and remember to keep your medallion safe, as you may have need of it again. Goodbye."

As Draco took flight once more, Huw and Ahmed saw two large helicopters approaching from the direction of the gorge. As they touched down, Colonel Kassim was the first to alight.

"Thank God, you are safe," he said, "and the horses too."

"We were in good hands," said Huw, "but what of Sheba and El Sufi?"

"They are both safely aboard the other helicopter," he said, "and now we must make our way back to the palace, where Sheikh Rashid is awaiting us. Will you come aboard?"

"No," said Huw and Ahmed in unison. "That is ... if you don't mind?" added Huw, somewhat sheepishly. "You see, Colonel, I think we would both prefer to ride back on these beautiful horses. It would be a kind of celebration gallop, if you know what I mean?"

Colonel Kassim smiled broadly and turned to board his helicopter once again.

Huw and Ahmed rode off towards the Palace, with hope in their hearts once more.

Chapter 27

The Royal Banquet

On June 1st, two weeks after Huw and the horses were rescued from their kidnappers, Sheikh Rashid announced that a banquet would be held on June 10th, at the Royal Palace, to celebrate their freedom from captivity. Huw had made a complete recovery, thanks to the nursing care he had received at the palace's medical centre. Normally, this was reserved for members of the royal family only, but Sheikh Rashid had insisted that Huw be given the best medical treatment available. Ahmed, Sheba and their grandfather had also been attended to and were all in good spirits. As for the horses, well, they were fed and watered, and pampered as never before. Fortunately they had not sustained any serious injury.

The banquet would be held in the Great Hall of the palace, and the Sheikh had announced that the guests of honour would be Huw, Arthur and Sam, Mary and Henry Grant, Huw's father Mike, who had been released from captivity in Dubai, Ahmed, Sheba and El Sufi – all of whom would sit at the top table.

Overseas guests would include the Prince of Wales and the Duchess of Cornwall, representing Queen Elizabeth II; the UK Foreign Secretary, John Hay; and the US Foreign Secretary, Pandora

Reiss. All the leaders of the Supreme Council of the UAE (United Arab Emirates) would be present, plus all religious leaders, and members of the Dubai Racing Club, including Saeed Ali. Senior Military Officers would include Colonel Kassim and Captain Maktar.

* * *

On the evening of June 10th, there was great excitement at the palace, as the guests of honour took their places at the top table in the Great Hall. Huw and his family sat to the right of Sheikh Rashid and Princess Serena. To the left sat Ahmed, Sheba and El Sufi. Stretching from the top table, two very long tables ran the full length of the Great Hall. To Rashid's right were seated the overseas guests, and to his left were the leaders of the UAE and others from neighbouring Arab and Muslim nations.

On this very special occasion, Sheikh Rashid had decided that the protocol would be different, and that the speeches and presentations would be made before the serving of the meal. As Sheikh Rashid rose to his feet, a great hush fell upon the Great Hall. To everyone present this was a heart-stopping moment.

"I am very pleased to welcome you all to the royal palace for this special occasion," said the Sheikh, "and especially our great guests of honour, who sit alongside me at the top table."

There was a magical moment of spontaneous applause from all the guests, and the Sheikh nodded in approval.

"Firstly, I wish to proclaim that Huw, Sam, Arthur, and Mr and Mrs Grant and Mr Pendry (Huw's father) are to become honoured citizens of Dubai, which of course, will give them many rights and privileges. This is in recognition of all they have done since the night of the terrible fire at the palace stables. I thought I would never see my beloved horse Ebony again, but thanks to the courageous acts of these visitors to our country, he is alive and well and will race again."

More applause.

"The young boy Huw has suffered greatly at the hands of the terrorists, but he has shown great spirit and resilience and survived his terrible ordeal. He will, from this moment, be treated as a foreign prince, whenever he visits our country. He will be known as the young Dragon Prince."

More applause.

"Also, I must give great praise to the young Bedouin boy and girl on my left: Ahmed and Sheba. Without their courage and fortitude, Huw, his father, and the horses would not have survived. Their grandfather, El Sufi, also displayed great wisdom and cunning to outwit the kidnappers. I have spoken to El Sufi, and with his permission, I have offered to adopt Ahmed and Sheba. They have agreed and will henceforward be known as Prince Ahmed and Princess Sheba."

Huge applause and loud cheering.

"El Sufi is to be appointed the new High Commissioner for all Bedouin peoples in the UAE."

More cheering.

"Colonel Kassim of the SDC (Special Desert Force) and Captain Maktar – of the Royal Guard – are to be awarded the Golden Heart Medal of Honour in recognition of their outstanding military leadership during this stressful period. I am relieved and pleased to say that all the terrorists have been arrested and are now awaiting trial. Their leader, known as Badrag, is no longer alive to stand trial, but died a horrible death when the wall of sand collapsed upon him. He who lives by the sword will die by the sword."

More applause.

"Lastly, I wish to announce, that next year there will be a new event in the Dubai Racing Calendar. This is being created in honour of our friends from the United Kingdom, and will be called the Pendragon Cup."

All the guests rose from their seats and there was loud cheering and prolonged applause following this final announcement.

Sheikh Rashid raised his hand; everyone became silent, and once more took their seats.

"And, now," he said, with a great big smile, "let the feast begin!"

Chapter 28

One Final Surprise

"What a fantastic banquet that was last night," said Sam, as they boarded the Chinook helicopter for a tour of the Dubai coastline. The trip had been specially arranged by Sheikh Rashid as a big surprise, and they were only told about it at breakfast.

"I thought Sheikh Rashid's speech was brilliant," said Huw, "and I can't believe he's made us all free citizens of Dubai."

"Not only that," said Arthur, "but he's asked us to stay here until it's time for us to go back to school in September."

"Look at the size of this helicopter!"

"Wow, do you know what this flight means! We'll get to see the famous hotel Burj El Arab, the one that looks like a giant sail and is actually higher than the Eiffel Tower in Paris."

"And what about all those new islands that they're building offshore?" said Sam. "One group looks like a Palm Tree, and the other like a huge Map of the World."

"This is the Captain speaking," said a familiar voice over the intercom. "Please fasten your seat belts and prepare for take off."

"That's Colonel Kassim," said Huw. "I'd recognise that voice anywhere."

"That's right," said the Captain's voice. "I can hear you too on this two-way radio system."

They all laughed loudly.

"And I'm here, too," said another familiar voice.

"That's Henry," said Arthur.

"Squadron Leader Henry Grant at your service."

Henry was momentarily drowned out by the roar of the engines, and the helicopter blades began to turn. Soon, they were rising from the helipad of the royal palace, and soaring westward towards the coast. They flew across the Al Maktoum Bridge, and then over the Dubai Creek, lined with Arab Dhows and luxury yachts. As the helicopter banked to the left, they had a bird's eye view of Port Rashid, where all the large oil tankers are handled. Then, they flew south-west along the Jumeira coastline, where they could see all the large hotels, including the famous Burj Al Arab. Far away to the east, they could see the peaks of the Hajar Mountains, and Huw felt a lump in his throat, when he recalled his days of captivity there. But now he was safe once more, and enjoying this magical tour of Dubai.

* * *

It was almost the end of August, when they returned home, as they all had to prepare for school on the 1st of September. Ahmed and Sheba also had to receive private tutoring, to prepare themselves for their new lives as adopted Prince and Princess. However, they were allowed to spend one week every month back in their Bedouin village, as well as during school holidays.

It was just before Christmas, when the vet informed Huw's

father Mike that Ivory was in foal. Mike ran to tell Mary and Henry and Sam the good news, and Sam ran as fast as her legs would carry her, to tell Huw and Arthur. They were all so excited, they could hardly contain themselves.

"Couldn't possibly have been Ebony, could it?" grinned Arthur wickedly. "Seems like the most likely suspect to me."

"Suspect for what?" said Sam innocently, without thinking.

"The foal's Dad, silly."

"Bit of a wild guess, Arthur," said Huw.

"Bet you a month's pocket money."

"OK, you're on," said Huw.

"That'll be enough, you two," said Mike. "First, we'll have to have some tests carried out, before we can assume anything."

"But what if the tests prove that the foal was sired by Ebony?" asked Huw.

"Well, we'll jump that hurdle when we come to it," said Mary, "and what we do will be my decision. So, until the time is right, no-one is to say anything about this outside these stable walls. Is that clear? I asked you – is that clear?"

"Perfectly clear," chorused everyone, "not a single word."

* * *

It was the 24th of March the following year, when Mary received a telephone call from Sheikh Rashid, telling her that Ebony had won the Dubai World Cup. He had sounded so jubilant, but Mary was still unable to tell him the news about Ivory.

On the 25th March, the day after the World Cup Race, the new foal was born. There was little doubt in anyone's mind now, as they all gathered in the stables of Grant Court to admire the young colt. He had the features and bearing of an Arab horse, and he was jet black with a white blaze on his face.

"Look," said Huw, "the blaze is shaped like a sword."

"So it is," said Mary, "and perhaps that will be the deciding factor in what his name should be." Then, she turned to Henry and Mike and said, "I think I would like the children to decide."

They both smiled and nodded their approval.

"The other thing is, that I think I would like to present him to Sheikh Rashid, as a special gift, to thank him for all he has done for us."

"Yes!" everyone shouted and cheered.

"I will go and call him now," said Mary, "while you decide on his name."

"I've got it," said Sam. "It has to be the name of King Arthur's sword."

"What, you mean …?"

"Yes," said Sam.

"But, how do you spell it?" asked Arthur.

"That's easy, peasy," said Sam, "X C a l i b u r, of course."

"X Calibur," they all cried.

* * *

"Well," said Mary, "that's a very modern spelling, but I like it, because he's certainly got the X factor. It's interesting that you should have chosen that name, because it may be more appropriate than you realize. I've been studying the latest research on King Arthur, and it seems as if he might have been descended from a horseman warrior, a knight who was sent to Britain from his native country, Sarmatia, by the Romans in the 5th Century."

"Where was Sarmatia?" asked Huw.

"Its roughly where Georgia is now: north of the Black Sea and south of Russia. So, you see, our links with the Middle East go back a long way."

"So, you think King Arthur was a descendant of these warriors."

"It seems very much like it, and there is evidence that one of the warriors was given the name Artorius. Not only that, but when he led his men into battle, he flew a windsock-like standard shaped like a dragon."

"But, what about the sword?"

"Well, there was a tribe of Sarmatians, who were known as the Kalybes, and they excelled in the making of white steel, which was known as Caliburn. The name Excalibur is believed to come from that."

"I still prefer my version of the spelling," said Sam.

"And why not?" said Mary. "I think I will go and make that phone call to Sheikh Rashid, and tell him the good news right away. He will be overjoyed."

As Mary left the stable, the others gathered around the beautiful young colt to admire him once more.

Probably another World Champion, thought Huw, just like his Dad.

"You owe me a month's pocket money," said Arthur, with a typical grin.

For a full list of Y Lolfa books currently in print, send now for your free copy of our new, full colour catalogue. Or simply surf into our website

www.ylolfa.com

for secure on-line ordering.

TALYBONT CEREDIGION CYMRU SY24 5AP
e-bost ylolfa@ylolfa.com
gwefan www.ylolfa.com
ffôn (01970) 832 304
ffacs 832 782